War

Lea Davies

War

Copyright © 2022 Lea Davies

ALL RIGHTS RESERVED

This book or any portion thereof must not be reproduced, stored in a retrieval system, or transmitted in any form or by any means (electronic, mechanical, photocopy, recording, scanning or other) without the express written permission of the author except for the use of brief quotations in a book review.

leadavies.com

The characters and events in this book are fictitious. Any similarity to real persons, dead or alive, is purely coincidental and not intended by the author.

War Is Book Three in The Vampire Ruth Series

Other books in the series

Book One: The Gift

Book Two: Choices

For my heart, my love, my life, my world, my John.

Acknowledgments

I want to thank everyone who helped me in the creation of this novella.

Firstly, my beautiful niece Janey, who was the first person to read Ruth and Matthew's story, and for giving me some great advice and encouragement.

Also, thank you to Felicia Darac and Clare Brown for giving me back my mojo when I needed it the most. I will be eternally grateful to you.

A big thank you also goes out to my good friends Martin and Caroline Payne, and the lovely Ella Taylor for proofreading my work, and for their unwavering enthusiasm. Also, to Derek Ryall and Rod Patient; Thank you guys for your kind words of encouragement; it meant a lot.

I would also like to say a big thank you to the incredible band that is POD (pain of death,) whose brilliant and atmospheric music was played continuously for inspiration while writing The Gift, Choices, and War.

And last but definitely not least, my amazing husband John, who was relentless in the pursuit of convincing me to tell Ruth and Matthew's story. Thank you, darling.

Before you read this novella, I thought it would be nice to enhance your reading experience by giving you a visualization of the characters as I imagine them to look, and so have created a short video for you to enjoy.
You can find them at leadavies.com/war

Happy reading.

Table of Contents

Introduction

Scene One: Sickening

Scene Two: Influence

Scene Three: Enlightenment

Scene Four: Reunited

Scene Five: Clean-up

Scene Six: Recruit

Scene Seven: Contentment

Scene Eight: Returned

Scene Nine: News

Scene Ten: Disbelief

Scene Eleven: Satisfaction

Scene Twelve: Hurt

Scene Thirteen: Surprise

Scene Fourteen: Dismissal

Scene Fifteen: Discussion

Scene Sixteen: Summoned

Scene Seventeen: Questioning

Scene Eighteen: Murder

Scene Nineteen: Discovery

Scene Twenty: Heartbreak

Scene Twenty-One: Parented?

Scene Twenty-Two: Suspicion

Scene Twenty-Three: Confrontation

Scene Twenty-Four: Devastated

Scene Twenty-Five: Approach

Scene Twenty-Six: Reveal

Scene Twenty-Seven: Fear

Scene Twenty-Eight: Mother

Scene Twenty-Nine: Uncaring

Scene Thirty: Knowledge

Scene Thirty-One: Disappointment

Scene Thirty-Two: Struggling

Scene Thirty-Three: Present

Scene Thirty-Four: Safety

Scene Thirty-Five: Sorry

Scene Thirty-Six: Gutted

Scene Thirty-Seven: Unremorseful

Scene Thirty-Eight: Fury

Scene Thirty-Nine: Pride

Scene Forty: Promise

Scene Forty-One: Anger

Scene Forty-Two: Test

Scene Forty-Three: Meeting

Scene Forty-Four: Relief

Scene Forty-Five: Trap

Scene Forty-Six: Fight

Scene Forty-Seven: Convincing

Scene Forty-Eight: Connection

Scene Forty-Nine: Love

Scene Fifty: Time

Scene Fifty-One: Determination

Scene Fifty-Two: War

Epilogue

About the Author

Other Books by Lea Davies

Introduction

Ruth begins her life with Matthew, but things quickly begin to spiral out of her control when Isabella Marshond parents her arch-nemesis, Jessica Bartlett, who once again, and this time as a vampire, vows to make her life a living hell.

War
Book three in the vampire Ruth series
By Lea Davies

Since Matthew lovingly bestowed me with "The Gift," some of our kind, (myself included) have made some bad "Choices," that have ultimately led us to "War."

Ruth Myers

He is he, and she is she.
Eyes meet, and he loves her.
She is dying, but he saves her.
Now he is she, and she is he.

Lea Davies

Scene One: Sickening

Isabella Marshond laid her hand on her new child's chest as she struggled to rise, and effortlessly held her naked body down on the bed where she had just awoken from completing her transformation into being a vampire. She bent and kissed her forehead before whispering in her ear. "As I promised," she purred, "I have a gift for you." Jessica's eyes darted across the room and landed directly on her father, who sat trembling on a deep red leather sofa.

"Do you still wish to make him suffer?" Isabella asked, smiling wickedly. Jessica licked her lips and looked deeply into her Uno Parente's eyes as she screamed in answer to her question. Isabella used her influence to control her. "Restrain yourself." She ordered.

"Why don't you take your time and play with him for a while? Think of *all* the things he did to anger you and make him pay. Remember that he chose to protect that dried-up old woman instead of supporting you, his own daughter."

She removed her hand from her chest and stepped back, and Jessica Bartlett rose menacingly from the bed. She clamped her narrowed eyes firmly on her terrified father's face and smiled as she slowly walked towards him. Isabella had influenced him to undress, be silent, and to sit still on her dark red leather sofa, but she hadn't told him not to be afraid. Tears ran down his face, and he shook with terror as the daughter he loved with all his heart approached, licking her lips hungrily. He whimpered when she inclined her head to the side, and paused to study him, then knelt at his feet and exposed her fangs for the first time.

Holding his eyes with hers, she smiled wickedly as she grabbed his foot, brought it up to rest on her shoulder, and licked along the skin on the inside of his leg, but Isabella interrupted, and Jessica looked up at her in confusion. "Do not lick him, my child," she cooed, "your saliva will numb his skin, and you said that you wanted him to suffer." Jessica's smile grew wider as she turned and looked back at her father.

Again, she held his eyes with hers as she playfully rested her newly formed fangs on his bare leg. She giggled childishly as she applied increasing pressure with every mock bite until she grew bored and sank her fangs deeply into his calf and ripped the muscle clean off the bone. Unable to scream or even to defend himself, his eyes opened wide as horrific pain coursed through his body, and she licked his blood as it poured from the wound.

Even though he had been influenced by the mother of all but one to remain silent, Joe Bartlett whimpered as his daughter took his limp penis in her hand and used it to pull herself forward. She parted his legs and maneuvered her body between them, then lowered her head to his stomach and put her mouth to it. The veins in his neck and temple bulged as she bit through the flesh and savagely tore it from his body; She spat the meat onto the floor and wiped the blood from her mouth with the back of her hand, then, in an instant, she straddled him and latched onto his throat, biting through the jugular vein, and drained him of any blood that still remained in his veins. His body shook uncontrollably as his life left him, and he became limp.

Isabella watched from across the room as her new child continued to bite all over her father's body and spit chunks of his flesh onto the floor, even after it was obvious that he was dead. She spat and snarled as she raked her fingernails deeply across his chest and screamed as she rubbed her father's blood all over her body.

Isabella's eyebrows drew together. "Hmm," she thought, "I did suggest that she should enjoy herself, but this is way beyond what I was expecting from her. This one was born wicked and will become a menace if not taken in hand."

She stepped forward and grabbed hold of her new child's arm. "That's enough, my dear," she said, and Jessica obediently got to her feet. Stephanie stepped forward and held out her hand. "Come with me," she said. "We need to get you cleaned up. You have a lot of work to do."

Isabella watched in silence as they walked past her, and before they had even left the room, she had already decided to end Jessica's existence once she had served her purpose.

Scene Two: Influence

After two long hours, Cathy Lester tried desperately not to laugh as she sat opposite Ruth at the kitchen table in number Twenty-Nine Sedan Street. Matthew glared playfully at her as he stood behind Ruth and rested both his hands on her shoulders. Shivers ran down her spine as his thumbs massaged her neck, and she closed her eyes and moaned with contentment. "Take your time," he said. "Concentrate, but don't try too hard."

She looked over her shoulder at him in confusion. "That doesn't make sense, Matt," she said, smiling. That was it. Cathy lost her battle and laughed, and both Ruth and Matthew joined her. "Alright, alright, that's enough," he said. "Come on, ladies. we have to concentrate." He looked at Ruth. "You have to take this seriously," he said. "If you don't, you won't be using your powers to their full potential, so you'll be perceived as being weak among the vampire community, and we can't have that, can we: I've got a rep to protect." He added with a smile.

She straightened her back and opened her mouth to make another joke, but Matthew cut her off. "Darlin', this is not a game," he said. "Come on; let's try again." Ruth knew he was right. Being able to influence people would be vital if she ever found herself in a tight spot and could even be the difference in a life-or-death situation.

She and Cathy rested their forearms on the table and leaned in towards each other. Cathy bit back a smile. "Try not to do that uni-brow thing," she said, waving her fingers across her forehead, and again, Matthew mock glared at her.

Ruth closed her eyes and honed in on her inner self. When she opened them, she concentrated on Cathy's face, and after a few moments, a tingling sensation that she had never experienced before rippled across the back of her neck and shoulders. The air seemed to stand still as she spoke. "Cathy," she said. "Stand up."

To both her and Matthew's surprise, the chair's legs scraped loudly across the laminate flooring as Cathy stood, put the flat of her hands on the tabletop, and stood.

Ruth chuckled, then laughed out loud. "Kiss, Matthew," she ordered. Matthew smiled and opened his arms wide as Cathy walked around the table and hugged her as she planted a kiss on his cheek. His face was full of pride as he looked at Ruth. "Tell her she has free will." He said, smiling. Ruth beamed. "You have free will, Cathy." She said.

Cathy blinked several times as if she were coming out of a deep sleep. She stepped forward and hugged Ruth warmly. "You did it, dear," she said. "I actually had no control over myself; I'm so proud of you." Ruth held her at arm's length. "Did I really do it?" she asked excitedly, "you weren't acting, were you?" Cathy's head shook emphatically. "Oh no dear," she said. "I promise you; You *really* did it." Ruth smiled as she pulled Cathy towards her in another hug. "How can I thank you for giving up your time to help me?" She asked. Cathy wiggled her eyebrows up and down mischievously. "Aren't you hungry yet dear," she asked. "It's been a few days since I fed you." Matthew covered his grin with his hand as he realised what she wanted.

"Come on then," Ruth giggled, "let's go downstairs, so you can lie comfortably on Matt's bed while I feed." Cathy turned and looked cheekily over her shoulder at Matthew and blew him a kiss. Her thick red wavy hair danced around her shoulders as she happily bounced down the stairs leading to the basement and followed Ruth to the bedroom.

Scene Three: Enlightenment

Ruth heard Matthews's car as he pulled into the driveway after taking Cathy home. She had said that she would get a cab, but he'd been on edge since his meeting with Isabella a few weeks ago and had insisted on driving her home himself. She, though, had come into full bloom. Her new abilities had given her the strength and confidence she had lacked in life, and as a result, she had what she called "grown a massive pair," and now, all of that would be significantly enhanced because she had just learned how to influence.

Somehow, Matt and Tori had skirted around the issue when she had tried to question them in depth about his Uno Parente, but tonight she had made up her mind to find out everything there was to know about her.

In a blur, she stood at the front door and opened it as he walked up the driveway and entered the house. He threw his arms around her and kissed her, but before the kiss grew deeper, she put the flat of her hands on his chest and gently pushed him away.

"Matt, we need to talk." She said. His voice was thick with passion. "After." He said, and again, pulled her to him. "the vampire rule book states that when your new child learns how to use her influence, you have to have celebration sex." She mock glared at him, and he pulled back, feigning indignity. "What you've accomplished here tonight Ruth, is epic." He said, biting back a smile. Ruth giggled and slapped his arm playfully. "Now you're just being silly." She laughed. The cheek of him; Using her ability to influence as an excuse to get her to sleep with him, was hilarious, but she cleared her throat and covered her face with a look that said she meant business.

"This is serious, Matt," she smiled. "I want to know more about your Uno Parente. All I know is what Tori told me before. That you worked closely together for a long time, and that Isabella had grown very fond of you. That's why I agreed with your sister when she said that she was worried that Isabella would be jealous of our relationship, but since then, every time I've asked you and Tori to tell me a bit more about her, you've both skillfully managed to change the subject. What are you hiding, Matt? I don't get why you avoid talking about her."

His face dropped, and he looked down at his feet. He agreed. This conversation was long overdue. "I know," he conceded, a tinge of worry in his voice. "OK. Let's talk." She followed him down the stairs to his basement bedroom, and they sat opposite each other at the same table they had sat at earlier with Cathy.

Ruth had a feeling that she wasn't going to enjoy this conversation but knew that it had to happen at some point. "Tell me everything there is to know about Isabella," she said. "Who is she, and what's the truth about your relationship with her?" This was it. Cards on the table time. "As you already know," he began, "she created me, *and*," he paused to clear his throat, "she was my lover for two centuries."

His words hit her like a sledgehammer. Although she knew that he must have had many lovers over the years, knowing that he and Isabella had had a long-standing relationship, hurt her. Tears formed behind her eye's, but she managed to hold them back, telling herself that he was entitled to have a romantic past with whoever he wanted. "Go on," she said, "start at the beginning."

Again, Matthew cleared his throat. "I first met her a few weeks before my twenty-first birthday," he continued, "but Ruth, when she parented me, I wasn't given a choice. She took my life without permission when she seduced me in her carriage, and I woke up alone in a cave, without guidance or any knowledge of where I was, or what I had become." She reached out, took his hand, and squeezed it with tender concern. "I can't imagine how terrifying that must have been for you." She said softly.

His eyes became distant as he remembered his awakening. "It was nowhere near as bad as it was for the poor man I fed on," he said sadly. "I managed to find my way home, and as I told you before, Tori was seriously ill with consumption, and it was obvious that she wouldn't last for much longer, so I revealed what had happened to me and what I had become. I offered her the choice to join me, and although she at first refused, she later agreed, and I parented her."

Remembering his sister dying in horrific agony because of his inexperience was painful for him to recall. By far, it was the worst memory he had of anything that had ever happened during his life, *or* death, and his eyes filled with tears. "You know the rest of the story," he said. He sat back in his chair, rubbed his eyes with the palms of his hands, then entwined his fingers at the back of his head. "I fed our bastard father to her for her first feed."

Ruth felt devastated for him. It must have been terrible for him to watch his twin die in so much pain. With his voice shaking, he leaned forward and rested his arms on the table.

"A few days later, Isabella came here to this house and helped teach Tori and me how to use our new abilities and to survive without bringing any unwanted attention to ourselves, and we became close. She told me that she hadn't parented me on a whim but had, in fact, watched me grow from a child into manhood. She trained me how to kill, and when it became evident that I had a natural talent for slaying, she made me chief executioner of unruly vampires. Still, it wasn't easy," he continued, "I had a lot to contend with. At first, a few of the council members thought that she chose me for the role purely because of her affection for me, so I worked hard to prove myself, and they eventually came to respect my position. I also had to put up with a lot of jealousy from vamps like Stephanie, the woman who came here a few weeks ago. She's been in love with Isabella for a long, long time and has openly resented me for years. She's never kept the fact that she doesn't think I deserve to be where I am a secret, but I'm telling you, Ruth, I've earned my position. No one is as good as me at hunting. I'm ruthless when it comes to destroying bad vamps, and I love my work." Pride covered his face, but then he smiled. "I have to admit, though; I haven't been on the ball recently; I've been a little distracted." He said with a twinkle in his eye.

Ruth threw him a warm smile. "Did Tori train too?" she asked. "She did," he replied proudly, "and as assassins go, she's one of the deadliest, which came as quite a surprise to me because she was such a gentle soul when she was alive. But things became a little strained when she told me that she could never forgive Isabella for taking my life without my consent and never felt completely comfortable around her. She thought that Isabella watching me as a little boy and waiting for me to grow up so that she could parent me was messed up, so it came as no surprise when she asked for missions that would take her to different parts of the world. She tried to convince me to go with her, but I chose to stay." "That must have been hard for you both," Ruth inserted. "Why did you stay? I thought that you two were inseparable."

He looked down at his hands. "I was besotted with her," he said candidly. "She is addicted to sex. She wants it morning, noon, and night. Can you imagine how that was for me, Ruth? There I was, a young man who had never had sex before, and suddenly I'm with this stunningly beautiful woman who wants it all the time. When she parented me, she gave me an eternal life that was both exciting and exhilarating, and to go alongside it, I had powers beyond belief, so yeah, I was besotted and wanted to be with her, so I stayed."

This was hard to hear. Ruth closed her eyes and took a moment. She had wanted him to be open, but she wasn't quite expecting him to be this frank.

"How did Tori react when you told her you were staying?" She asked. Guilt covered his face. "She was heartbroken," he said, "she even refused to have any contact with me for a few years, but thankfully, after a while, she came to accept the situation, and we arranged to meet up here, in the home we grew up in, between missions."

Her eyes widened with surprise. "You grew up here?" She asked. "Yeah," he said, "but I only come here every couple of years. I don't think it's wise to stay in the same place for an extended period of time because the people around you generally seem to notice when you don't age at the same rate as they do," he chuckled softly, "but I've been lucky here. People usually tend to keep to themselves, and the houses in this street have changed hands quite often over the years, so I haven't really had to worry about it too much."

Ruth gave him a half-smile. "Well, you learn new things about the people you love every day, don't you." She said. He got the underlying message loud and clear. She wasn't only referring to Sedan Street being his childhood home. She was talking about what he had told her about his Uno Parente being his lover for such a long time.

He reached across the table and, again, took her hand in his. He wanted this conversation to be over and done with, but not if it was going to hurt her. "Do you want me to carry on?" He asked. "I can see that this is upsetting you, darlin'. Shall we at least take a break?" She shook her head. "Some of this is really hard to hear, Matt," she admitted, "but hear it, I must, so, carry on. Tell me everything." Matthew braced himself. None of the rest of this conversation was going to be pleasant.

"Isabella once even told me that she loved me," he continued, "but to tell you the truth, I don't know if she's capable of truly loving anyone or anything, but as far as I'm aware, I'm the closest person that has ever come to it." Considering that Isabella was ancient and had undoubtedly had countless opportunities to fall in love but had not, Ruth found the accolade quite staggering.

"When did your relationship end?" She asked. Matthew sighed. "It was never what you would call a "relationship," Ruth. We both slept with other people, so it wasn't as if we were exclusive to each other. What we had was purely sexual. It's been well over a year since I've even seen or had any sort of contact with her, but in answer to your question, any desire I had for her *or* anyone else ended when I met you." She looked at him for a long moment, and he felt that he could almost hear the cogs of her brain going into overdrive.

"Did you love her?" She asked, dreading his reply. He lowered his voice and leaned across the table. "I can honestly tell you, Ruth, that I have never, ever been in love with anyone for as long as I've been on this earth, alive or dead. Not until I met you anyway." He added. He reached out and touched her face tenderly.

"Does she know that you're in love with me?" She asked. He gave her a sexy, lopsided grin. "Yes, she does," he said, nodding his head, "when I met with her, she at first said that my decision to parent you had come from between my legs, but I told her that she was wrong and that I loved you." She relaxed a little and smiled. Her eyes were moist with unshed tears.

"What's Isabella's story?" She asked. "Where is she from?" Matthew pursed his lips. "The only thing I can tell you for sure is that she's thousands and thousands of years old. She often refers to herself as the mother of all but one, but I don't understand what that means, and to be honest, I don't think there's anyone that does," he said. "It's something that she point-blank refuses to clarify. I was present when two council members who were known to be her closest, and most trusted allies, grew overconfident in their relationship with her and asked who her mother was and what that phrase meant."

He shook his head slowly as he recalled the memory. "It did *not* go well for them, Ruth. It was absolutely horrific." "What do you mean?" she asked. "Did she kill them?" He nodded his head emphatically. "Oh yeah," he said, "she *really, really* killed them. She influenced them to attack, and bite chunks out of each other, then when she grew bored with the spectacle, she decapitated them, and they disintegrated into dust right before my eyes. That incident and a few others like it are the reason why her volatile nature is legendary among vampires."

Butterflies flew around her stomach. She knew that at some point, she would have to meet this woman and dreaded the thought. "She can influence other vampires," She said in wonder. "I had never thought about whether one vamp could do that to another one." "They can't," he said. "As far as I'm aware, she's the only one capable of doing it, and that's what makes her even more dangerous." "I'm a little confused," she said. "I didn't think that she did cruel things like that. I just thought she was an old and very powerful vampire who ran the council and has vampire assassins, like yourself, to protect the human race." He looked uncomfortable as he answered. "Oh no," he said, "you're way off the mark. The council wasn't created to protect the human race; it was created to protect vampires."

Shaking her head in surprise, Ruth let go of his hand and sat back in her seat. "Do you think she would have reacted like that if it were you who had asked her who her mother was?" She asked, her voice tinged with worry. He shook his head. "I honestly can't answer that," he said, "all I can tell you, is that if anyone else had spoken to her the way that I did at our meeting, she would have ended them on the spot, but with me, she showed leniency and let me off with a warning. I don't honestly know whether she did that because of her fondness for me or whether there's something else going on. Something bad, which is why I said that you, Tori, and I should keep our guards up.

He saw her concern and wished that he didn't have to remind her of that conversation. "Try not to worry too much, Ruth." He said, trying to ease the tension. Unfortunately, frown lines ran along her forehead, and it became evident that his attempt to placate the situation had not been entirely successful.

Scene Four: Reunited

As the girl beneath him moaned and moved her body to meet his every thrust, Jason Hardwick's eye's squeezed tightly shut as he cried out and climaxed. Without emotion or even the slightest consideration for the woman in his bed, he rose and put on a pair of boxer shorts that he really should have changed days ago and left the room. He picked up the jeans he had draped over a kitchen chair earlier in the evening and rifled around in the pockets for his tobacco pouch. He took it out, removed a cigarette paper and a good pinch of tobacco, and made a cigarette. He lit it and inhaled deeply, appreciating the rich warmth of the smoke as it filled his lungs. He picked a loose strand of tobacco from his tongue as he exhaled, then turned when he heard the knock on his front door.

"Who the fuck is that?" He sneered as he walked to see who was there. "It's one o fucking clock in the morning." He opened the door, and his face dropped when he saw Jessica standing there. He thought that her father had carried out his threat to send her away because he hadn't seen her for weeks, and to be honest, he was glad of it. Her behaviour was getting worse, and she was starting to get even on his nerves. "Have you missed me, baby?" she asked seductively.

The smile disappeared when she noticed his eyes look fleetingly towards his bedroom door. She casually placed her hands on the architrave at each side of the doorway and tilted her head to the side as she concentrated on his face. "Invite me in." She ordered. He looked a little puzzled as he stepped back and held the door open wide. "Come in." He said nervously.

As she stepped over the threshold, her eyes landed directly on the skirt and halter neck top lying discarded on the floor. She turned and put her hand on his manhood, then rubbed it sensuously. "I guess that's a no then," she said when he failed to become erect. "You've been gone a while," he said. "I moved on."

Both heads turned as the bedroom door opened, and a naked woman appeared. She took one look at Jessica and immediately stepped back inside the room and closed the door behind her. Jessica sneered. "So I see," she said.

She stepped forward and snatched the freshly made roll-up from his fingers. "Get rid of her." She ordered, and without question, he opened the bedroom door and told his new lover to leave. Tears streamed down the girl's face as she begged him not to make her go, and Jessica raised her eyebrows when she heard her tell him that she loved him. "Get a grip, you stupid fucking bitch," she shouted. "You've only fucking known him for five minutes. Believe me; I'm doing you a fucking favour, so piss off, and for your own safety, don't you ever come back."

The woman angrily snatched up her underwear and put it on; then, she walked into the kitchen and bent to pick up the rest of her clothing from the floor. Jessica's eyes narrowed as she watched her dress. If it weren't for the fact that Stephanie would tell Isabella what she had done, she would have murdered the girl the moment she walked into the room, but Isabella had a strict rule about not killing people, so she thought it would be wise to hold her temper. She didn't want to piss her Uno Parente off.

The woman hastily stepped into her skirt, and as soon as the halter was over her head, she turned, crossed the room, stood directly in front of Jessica, and glared. Instantly, she fell to her knees and hyperventilated as her love rival hissed and bared her fangs in her face. As she struggled to catch her breath, Jessica grabbed her arm and dragged her across the room, where she unceremoniously threw her out onto the concrete balcony and spat on her face before slamming the door shut.

Jason Hardwick's entire body shook with terror as she turned to face him. She smiled menacingly as she spoke. "Now," she said, walking towards him, "where were we?"

Scene Five: Clean-up

Stephanie Mercer stood silently in the coolness of the concrete staircase and waited patiently for the woman on all fours outside Jason's door to regain control of her breathing. She agreed with her lover; Jessica was a loose cannon. It was a good job that Isabella had suggested that she accompany her to enlist her boyfriend as a human helper tonight because she suspected that someone would be needed to clean up any mess she left in her wake. Still, it would be worth it; Jason Hardwick could prove invaluable to them in their campaign to destroy Ruth and Matthew.

Because of the state she was in, it was glaringly obvious that Jessica had revealed herself to the woman and had neglected to influence her to forget. It came as no surprise to Stephanie that her new abilities had quickly gone to her head, but she had had to admit that she had taken to them like a duck to water.

In a blur, Stephanie stood and hovered over the young woman on the floor. She bent and held out her hand.

"Here, let me help you up," she said softly. Still in a fit of panic, the woman tried to scamper away, so Stephanie used her influence. "Don't be afraid," she said. "You will not be harmed." Calmness covered her face, and she smiled as Stephanie turned and walked away. "Follow me." She said over her shoulder.

When they reached the cover of the staircase, Stephanie gently guided the woman to the wall and held her there; then, she lowered her hand to her most intimate area. "One bite won't hurt," she thought. "I just want a small taste."

She licked her lips. "Remain calm." She

purred. As her hand worked between the woman's legs, she pulled the hair away from her neck and turned her head to the side, then slid her tongue along the skin to numb the area and released fang serum into the wound as she drank. The woman's legs shook, and she grabbed onto Stephanie's arms as she moaned in ecstasy.

Taking care not to take too much, Stephanie removed her fangs from the woman's throat and waited patiently for her orgasm to subside.

"When you wake up in the morning, you will remember nothing that has taken place here this evening." She said. "The puncture wounds on your throat will be of no concern to you, and you will not even give them a second thought, do you understand?" The woman nodded. "Wear a scarf around your neck until they have completely healed, OK? Now, go home like a good girl, and forget all about Jason Hardwick. He's nothing but a piece of shit and is not the man for you." She ordered, wiping the blood away from the corners of her mouth with her thumb and forefinger.

Again, the woman nodded, then calmly walked over to the lift, pressed the call button, and waited patiently for it to arrive. Stephanie smiled inwardly. Still, to this day, she marvelled at the power of influence.

Scene Six: Recruit

Jason Hardwick's back was stiff with tension as he sat next to his ex on his old worn-out sofa. Jessica pulled a loose strand of material from its fraying cover, then spoke. "You," she said, "will be my eyes and ears during the daylight." He nodded but remained silent. He found it hard to believe that she was a vampire but knew that he couldn't deny what his eyes had seen.

"Who was that slut I just threw out?" She asked. "I heard her say she loved you; is that true? Do you have feelings for her, or was she just someone to fuck while I wasn't around?" She hissed and bared her fangs as Jason shook uncontrollably. "If you do," she continued, "I might just have to fucking eat her."

Tears fell from his eyes as she threw her head back and laughed at his terror. The Jason that she had known and shagged on a regular basis was afraid of nothing and no one. Seeing him like this disgusted her, but then a flashback of Ruth confronting her in the alley flooded her mind, and she retracted her fangs.

She rose, stood directly in front of him, and slowly removed her tight black leather trousers, crop top, and panties. His hands held onto her hips as she straddled him. "Get hard." She ordered, and within moments, he was ready for her. She leaned forward and nibbled on his ear as she moved up and down. "After this," she said, "we're gonna pay Suzie Price a visit, but for now, I want you just to relax and enjoy the ride."

He laid his head on the back of the sofa as lust swept through his body, but it wasn't enough to dispel his terror. Fresh tears from the corner of his eyes ran down his temples and pooled in his ear. "There there," she said as again, she hissed and exposed her fangs. "Don't be afraid; I'll only have a little nibble."

Scene Seven: Contentment

Matthew kissed Ruth tenderly, and she sighed with contentment. "I can't remember my life without you in it," she said. "I feel so happy. Everything's working out well with my family, and I even think that my mum fancies you a tiny bit." Matthew nodded. "Yeah," he chuckled. "I got that feeling too." His smile faded a little. "I still feel bad about using my influence to get Beth and Jack to take her in for the unforeseeable future, though." Ruth nodded. "I know," she said, "but you shouldn't feel too bad about it. There was a really good chance that that would have happened anyway."

She smiled and lightly bit her lower lip. "If I were you," she said, "I would take comfort in knowing that you didn't need to use the influence when I told her that I was moving in with you. She was happy for me." He kissed her again. "There you go," he said. "You're doing what you always do." She looked puzzled. "What do you mean, doing what I always do?" He leaned closer and laid his hand on her naked thigh. "Making everyone around you feel better about themselves." He said. "What can I say?" She smiled. "It's what I do, oh, and while we're on the subject of my family," she said, "don't forget that we promised to visit them all this evening. His voice was hoarse with passion as he slid his hand up along the inside of her leg. "Later." He whispered.

Scene Eight: Returned

Suzie Price finished her bedtime routine and got into her bed. She picked up the TV remote, pressed the red button, and the TV came to life. She scrolled through several different channels before landing on a reality program she wanted to watch, then, reaching over to her nightstand, she opened the drawer and took out the half-eaten bar of chocolate she had opened the night before. Her mouth watered as she nestled her back into her pillows, neatly broke off the first piece, and popped it into her mouth. She felt happy and content.

Earlier, she had gone to an induction session at her new college and had plucked up the courage to talk to a boy from her neighbourhood that she had always liked but had never dared to approach, and at the end of the session, he had asked her if she wanted to meet up for a drink. Her confidence had grown tenfold since Jessica had not been on the scene, and she distantly wondered where she was. "Had her father sent her away?" She thought, but it didn't explain why Jessica had made no attempt to call her. Whatever had happened, she hoped that it would stay that way.

Her hand stopped halfway to her mouth when she heard a light tap on her window, but she ignored it, thinking it must be the wind, but when she heard the second tap, she got out of bed to take a look. Her heart sank when she saw Jessica and her boyfriend Jason looking up at her from where they stood in the Price's back garden. "Get down here, you stupid cow," she called. "I need to talk to you."

Suzie felt thoroughly miserable as she nodded and dropped the bedroom curtain back into place, and turned to walk down the stairs. "Sooz," Jessica cooed as she opened the back door. "come outside." Suzie felt as if she were in a dream as she stepped barefoot onto the grass. "I'm glad you're here," she said. "I thought your dad had sent you away for good."

Jessica folded her arms across her chest in annoyance. "Don't fucking lie," She snapped. "I can't stand liars, and you know it." Suzie tried to plead her innocence and did her best to look sincere. "Where have you been, Jess?" She asked. "I've been worried."

A mischievous smile covered Jessica's cruel face. "I've been busy," she answered. "Busy doing what?" Suzie asked. Jessica's smile grew wider, pleased with how she had expertly led her friend towards asking that particular question. She hissed and bared her fangs as she stepped closer. "Busy dying." She said.

Suzie gasped and clutched her chest. She fell to her knees, toppled forward, and was dead before her head hit the floor. "Fucking pussy," Jessica said with disgust. "I can't fucking believe that I let you hang around with me; you didn't even come looking for me to see if I was alright after I had that run-in with Ruth outside the club, did you."

She looked down at Suzie's body and felt no remorse for the loss of her friend. In fact, all she felt was disappointment that she wouldn't be able to use her as another set of eyes and ears. She filled her mouth with saliva, and spat on Suzie's back, then turned to leave but stopped dead in her tracks and smiled wickedly as a new plan formed in her mind.

Scene Nine: News

The mood was good as all but Ruth and Matthew ate fish and chips from the cardboard boxes sat on their laps. Beth leaned forward and held her box of food out in front of them. "Are you sure you don't want a chip?" She asked. "Honestly, I've got too many. Bert's portions are way too big for me." Ruth bit back a smile. "No thanks, Beth," she said, sharing a private look with Matthew. "We ate earlier."

Beth sat back in her chair. "Turn the TV on, Jack," she said. "The news is coming on; let's see what's going on in the world." Jack wiped the grease from his mouth and hands with a paper napkin, picked up the TV remote, and switched it on.

"The exsanguinated remains of the body found on Povey estate, southeast London last week," the news anchor said solemnly, "have been identified as those of Jeremy Weller, a well-known local criminal." They watched as front and side-view mugshots of Lesley's attacker holding an identification plaque to his chest appeared on the screen.

Lesley's hand flew to her mouth, and tears filled her eyes. "What's wrong, mum?" Ruth asked. "That's him," she answered, pointing at the TV screen. "That's the man who attacked me."

Matthew glared at Ruth, and she knew what he was thinking. No one noticed as she slightly shook her head in denial, but Matthew excused himself and left the room. Ruth didn't follow him. She was beyond angry to think that he could even consider her to be responsible for killing Jerry Weller. She went to her mother and laid her arm around her shoulders.

Lesley's eyes grew into slits as she looked down at the pureed food in her bowl. "I know it's a wicked thing to say," she said, "but good bloody riddance. That man was the nastiest piece of work you could ever want to meet, so I'm not at all surprised that his life has ended violently."

Beth knelt on the floor in front of her sister. "Les, now that it's out in the open," she said, "what happened?" Lesley hung her head in shame as she remembered her past behaviour. The last thing she wanted was for her daughter to hear what she was about to reveal, but knew there was no way she could avoid it. "He was my pimp," she said, "and he did this to me because I held back some of his money, and he found out."

Ruth noticed that Callie was staring at her. "Is she thinking the same as Matthew?" she thought, but her cousin gave her a half-smile. "Are you OK?" Callie mouthed silently, and

Ruth realised that she was only showing concern for how she would react to her mother's news. She nodded and returned the smile. Jack broke the silence. "That man was a coward for beating you the way he did," he said. "Well, they say that you reap what you sow, so it sounds like he got exactly what he deserved."

Scene Ten: Disbelief

Matthew paced at the end of the driveway as she came out of the house to confront him. "I can't believe that you would even think that," Ruth said. She poked her chest as she spoke. "If you really loved and trusted me as much as you say you do, then that thought would never have entered your head; I didn't even know who he was until just now. I asked my mother who attacked her when she was still in the hospital, but she refused to tell me. Did you hear her say what a nasty piece of work he was? There must be a whole line-up of people out there who would hate him enough to have killed him."

Matthew's anger bubbled over, and he couldn't hold it in. "You can't blame me," he said. "The reporter said that he'd been drained of blood; what conclusion would you have come to if you were me? It's not as if you haven't gone off the rails before, is it," he said, "you know how to influence now; Did you use it on your mother to find out who he was?"

She felt as if he had punched her full in the gut. "Are you always going to hold my past mistakes over my head, Matt? She whispered heartbrokenly. She turned and walked back up the pathway to the house. "I think you had better leave," she said over her shoulder. "Right now, I don't want you anywhere near me." "Ruth." He called after her, but she was already inside the house.

Scene Eleven: Satisfaction

Stephanie Mercer smiled to herself as she crouched down in her car on the opposite side of the road and eavesdropped on Ruth and Matthew's heated discussion. Isabella had been right when she had said, "divide and conquer." So far, it seemed to be working a treat."

Both parties looked broken as they turned and went their separate ways, but she had enjoyed the spectacle. She had always hated Matthew with a passion and enjoyed it when things didn't go right for him.

She smiled as she sat up in her seat and turned the key in the ignition. After spending all of her life, and most of her death in the background, she was now exactly where she wanted to be and was doing what she had always wanted to do. Isabella had taken her to her bed many times since she had first reported her findings on Matthew and his whore, and she was now regarded by her lover's many guards and hangers-on, and even some members of the council, as one of her closest confidants.

She couldn't wait to get back to the mansion to tell Isabella what she had just seen and that their plan was working beautifully. She fantasized about them making love and licked her lips seductively as she pulled the car out onto the road.

Scene Twelve: Hurt

Stephanie thumbed the button on the key fob Isabella had given her, and the hinges on each of the large electric gates groaned as they opened and closed behind her shortly after. She drove as close as she could get to the house, and threw the keys to the large suited man who approached her as she got out of the car.

"Where's Isabella?" She asked. He nodded curtly at one of the downstairs windows, then grinned. "In bed." He said. "What are you smiling about?" She asked, annoyed at his attitude. His grin grew wider. "You'll soon see." He said. He got into the car and drove it to a garage situated at the rear of the property. Her eyes narrowed as she watched him pull away. After reporting to Isabella, she promised herself that she would personally see to it that he would be made fully aware of her new status beside the mother of all but one.

She climbed four two-meter wide, brick-built steps that led into the mansion and walked directly to Isabella's bedroom. Her ears pricked up when she heard familiar noises coming from within, and before she could stop herself, she entered the room without knocking. Jessica's back was arched in rapture as she held the head of the only person that Stephanie had ever loved between her legs. She was rooted to the spot.

The whites of her knuckles showed through the pale skin as her hands balled into fists. Isabella raised her head and looked in her direction. "Wait outside the door," she said, "We've only just started, so we may be some time." "But Isabella," she inserted, "could I not join you?" Isabella returned to her work between Jessica's legs, and casually dismissed her from the room with the flick of her hand.

Glassy-eyed, Jessica raised her head from the pillow, looked at her, and smiled wickedly. At that moment, Stephanie Mercer vowed to do whatever it took to destroy her in the most horrendous way that she possibly could.

Scene Thirteen: Surprise

Tori couldn't believe what Matthew had just told her. "What," she asked, wide-eyed, "surely you can't think that Ruth did that." He glanced at her sideways. "I don't want to think it, Tor, but the man's body had been completely drained of blood. After the way she behaved before, what would you think?"

Tori had to admit he had a point. Ruth had schemed and blatantly lied to them, so she could empathise with his way of thinking.

"Why can't you just trust her word?" she asked, "she hasn't put a foot wrong these past few weeks has she." Matthew closed his eyes with impatience. "No, she hasn't," he said, "but this involves her mother," he said, "still, to this day, I remember how full of rage I was when you told me that our father had laid his hands on you, and you remember how I reacted to that don't you?"

She nodded but stayed quiet, purely because she couldn't think of what to say in Ruth's defence. "All the while he was beating me to a pulp, I weathered it through, but when he slapped you, it became a completely different matter. Don't you think that there's a good chance that she may have reacted in the same way?"

Tori stood and faced him. "I can't answer that, Matt," she said, "but you need to go back and talk to her; We need to figure this out. "I will," he said, "but not tonight."

Scene Fourteen: Dismissal

Isabella sat behind her desk in the orangery and smiled as her new child approached. Although she was impressed with the girl's wickedness and determination to destroy Matthew's whore, and was also an excellent bed partner, Isabella still considered her to be unstable, and her decision to end her after it was over had not changed.

"Where have you put the body?" She asked. Jessica grinned. "I didn't want it to stink up the place, so I stuck it in my boyfriend's freezer," she replied casually. Isabella smiled inwardly, pleased with how everything seemed to be neatly falling into place. "When do you want me to drop it off around Matthew's house?" Jessica continued. "I can't wait to get the ball rolling. I want to see the look on that smug bitch's face when she sees it. I'm gonna make her pay for what she fucking did to me in the alley that night. She's not gonna know what hit her when I'm done with her."

Stephanie had reported that as expected, Matthew and his whore had argued when the discovery of Jerry Weller's exsanguinated body had reached the local news headlines. She knew that it would only be a matter of time before he realised that she was innocent but was hoping that the whore would hold his accusations against him, and cracks would appear in their relationship.

She chuckled. "They must be going through hell right about now," she thought, "I wish I could be a fly on the wall so that I could watch them suffer." "Good," she said, "You have done well, and I am very pleased with your progress."

Jessica moved closer, and the guards to

either side of Isabella stepped forward and blocked her path as she neared. Isabella casually waved them aside then dismissed them altogether. Apart from her mother, she was the most dangerous creature on the planet, so it wasn't as if she needed them. Still, since the attempt that Seth Ahmed had made on her life, she had taken extra precautions to keep herself safe. She realised that albeit slight, there was a chance that someone could possibly discover that a stake through the heart *could* kill her, but it had to be a special one. But anyway, they looked impressive and often came in handy when she felt the need for sexual satisfaction.

Stephanie watched from across the room as her love rival straddled Isabella's knee, and she began to grind herself against her. Sickened by the sight, she stepped forward and loudly cleared her throat. "Isabella," she said, "what's our next move?" She was ignored as Isabella pulled Jessica's tee-shirt up over her head and dropped it on the floor, then teased her child's nipples with her tongue and teeth. Jessica's head fell backward, and she moaned.

Desperate to stop what was happening in front of her, Stephanie stepped even closer and again, loudly cleared her throat. "Isabella, we should discuss our next move, don't you think?"

Since Jessica had been on the scene, Isabella had not once invited her to her bed. Of course, she was under no illusion that she would ever be in an actual relationship with her, but she had come to think of herself as being one of Isabella's favourites.

"Isabella," she pleaded, but her words fell on deaf ears. In an act of desperation, she moved behind Isabella, removed her clothing, and rubbed herself against the woman she loved. Isabella's fangs flashed angrily as she spun around and threw Stephanie across the room.

Cracks appeared as she crashed into a wall

made of thick glass bricks. Her heart shattered into a million pieces as blood filled her mouth. The lump that formed in her throat was so huge that she knew that if she had still been alive, she wouldn't have been able to breathe. Jessica made no attempt to hide the enormous grin covering her face.

"Take a fucking hint, you stupid bitch." She laughed. At that moment, her heart truly broke, and she felt as if she had died for the second time in her life as Isabella sneered and coldly waved her from the room.

Scene Fifteen: Discussion

Ruth paced the floor in front of her cousin. "He's gonna have to come to me first," she said, furiously jabbing her finger into her chest, "my days of being servile are well and truly over, and I'm not saying that because of my new strength," she continued, "before I transformed, I had already vowed to grow a pair, remember?"

Biting back a smile, Callie nodded as she recalled Ruth swearing in the changing room on the day Beth had bought her a sexy new outfit to wear to the nightclub. It seemed like it was such a long time ago.

Ruth sat next to her cousin on the bed and turned to face her. "Since that terrible night in the alley," she paused and looked guiltily at

Callie as she remembered the events of that night in all its shocking glory, and she gently rubbed her cousin's arm in another silent apology. "I've controlled myself and have learned how to use my abilities properly," she continued. "but obviously, Matthew still has his doubts about me, so I don't know what else I can do to convince him that he has nothing to worry about." Her lip quivered. "I love him so much, Cal, and can't bear the thought of losing him, but how can we be together in a loving relationship if he doesn't trust me? I know that what I did was unforgivable, especially to you, but I'm trying to put it behind me and get on with my life."

Again, she stood and paced the floor. Thinking back to that night brought Jessica to mind, and her agitation grew. In the past few weeks, Ruth had been able to resolve herself to the fact that although she had got the fright of her life, Jessica had gotten away with what she had done to her. In actuality, she had gotten away with murder.

Anger ran riot through her body, but she quickly used a simple technique that Tori had taught her to dampen it down. She closed her eyes and imagined a large field filled with flowers not yet come into bloom. A light, gentle breeze kissed the surface of the ground, as one by one, she pictured them opening, one petal at a time. After a few moments, she could see each flower with such clarity that she actually found herself smiling. She couldn't believe that Tori's technique worked as well as it did and would be eternally grateful to her. "Thank you, Tor." She said to herself.

Significantly calmer, Ruth opened her eyes and sighed. She knew she had to break the deadlock. "I have to go and speak to him, don't I," she conceded as she sat back down on the bed. Callie nodded in agreement. "'Fraid so," she said. She paused and briefly considered her next words. Matthew's summarization had already hurt her cousin, and she didn't want to upset her any further, "I don't want to piss you off, Ruth," she started, "but maybe you should look at it from his side because I kind of understand where he's coming from, I mean, you did go after Jessica."

Ruth nodded slowly as the truth dawned on her. She realised that she couldn't really blame Matthew for thinking the way he did, but still, she felt that he should have trusted her. Her lip trembled, and Callie reached out and gently placed her hand on her cousin's arm. "Why don't you bite the bullet and pay him a visit. Staying out of each other's way isn't solving anything, is it." She pressed.

Ruth knew she was talking sense. "Anyway, you have to find out who killed Jerry Weller, don't you?" She added. Ruth agreed; This was no time for petty arguments. If she could find his killer, she could also prove her innocence. "Also," Callie continued, "aren't you worried that Matthew's, what did you call her, parenty? Knows about Weller's death; She might have come to the same conclusion as Matthew did and think that you had something to do with it."

Despite the butterflies fluttering in her stomach at the mention of Isabella, Ruth showed the hint of a smile. "You mean his Uno Parente," she said, trying to lighten the tone. "It means single parent in Latin. I suppose it makes sense because when you're born into the world the way that nature intended, you have two parents, but it only needs one vampire to bite and turn you, so yeah, single parent fits the bill."

She laughed as Callie's eyebrows drew together. "Who's doing the uni-brow thing now." She giggled. Callie laughed with her. "Surely they could have come up with a better name than that," she teased. "How about mummy biter or daddy sucker?" She suggested with a grin. She Leaned forward, hissed, stuck out her top teeth, and curled her hands into claws in front of her face. "How about nibbler?" she asked, laughing hysterically, "or even dribbler, you know, for when the blood runs down their chin?" Ruth chuckled, then laughed out loud. She was impressed by how far her cousin had come since fainting when Matthew showed her his fangs for the first time.

"Very funny, Cal," she giggled, "I'll put it to the council, shall I? Let's see how they feel about swapping Uno Parente for dribbler." Callie's eyes opened wide in mock terror. "No, don't you dare do that." She joked. "Let's just keep it between us. I don't want any of them coming around here and flashing their fangs at me thank you very much. I've seen yours and Matt's, and that was enough to last me a lifetime."

Both women laughed, but after a few moments, Callie cleared her throat. Her smile gone, she spoke with concern. "Well?" She pressed, "*are* you worried about her?" Ruth shrugged. "To tell you the truth," she said, "the thought that Isabella could come to the same conclusion as Matt *has* crossed my mind, but I'll worry about that when or if it happens."

Deeply disappointed at the way things were turning out, she looked down at her feet and sighed. When Matthew saved her and her mother came back into her life, she thought that all the misery she had gone through in the past year was over, but now there was this. She stood and placed a light kiss on her cousin's cheek. "Oh well," she said resignedly, "I suppose I should go and get this over with. See you later, Cal."

Scene Sixteen: Summoned

Matthew rubbed his eyes as he sat up in the bed and focused on the girl sitting in the armchair across the room from him. His smile was one of love and warmth as Ruth suddenly appeared by the bed, lifted the sheet, and got in next to him.

"I'm still not talking to you," she whined. "and I am *not* your friend." She pouted and shot him a look that had him playfully scoot away from her. "Don't worry," he said, mocking in his voice, "I'm not yours either."

He smiled and lifted his arm, so she moved closer to him and nestled in. "Even though he did those terrible things to my mother, do you seriously think I had anything to do with the death of that vile man?" she asked. "As angry as I am, I'm still the same person that I was in life. I wouldn't hurt a fly, Matt. "

"You went after Jessica." He said flatly. Rolling her eyes, she huffed a sigh of frustration. "Yes, I did," she argued, "but I didn't go after her with the intent to kill her, Matt; I only wanted to humiliate her and to make her wish that she was dead because that's how she made me feel. There were days when I just wanted to go to sleep and never wake up again."

Matthew was gutted by what she had just told him. He lifted her chin with his finger and held her eyes with his. "She made you feel that you wanted to die?" He asked. "I'm so sorry, darlin'." She sighed and nodded, surprised when she felt tears in her eyes. A faint smile brushed her lips as she wiped them away with the sleeve of her tee-shirt. "I've never actually admitted that to myself before now," she said, "but that's honestly how she made me feel, Matt; Like I didn't want to be here anymore."

Considering the other issue she had had to contend with concerning her mother, he wasn't at all surprised that she felt that way; still, he wanted to explain why he had thought she might have been involved with Jerry Weller's death and to discuss an even bigger issue that worried him.

"I know that you didn't go there with the intention to kill her, Ruth," he gently conceded, "but you must admit that if Tori and I weren't there to stop you, you would have taken it much further. Admit it; You had lost all control." Ruth sighed as she surrendered to the truth.

"The thing that really worries me, though," he continued, his voice taut with nervous tension, "is what Isabella and the council will think. Don't forget that they know about what happened in the alley that night with Jessica. They will have used their eyes and ears to find out everything there is to know about you and your family and will know about the connection between Jerry Weller and your mother, so if *I* can think you capable of killing him, then *they* can do the same." Ruth stood from the bed and chewed her nails as she paced the floor.

They turned as they heard Tori descend the stairs to the basement, and a sense of unease filled the room when they saw the look on her face. "What's wrong, Tor?" Matthew asked. "Stephanie is here again," she said solemnly, "Isabella has summoned you to come immediately, and she's here to escort you to the mansion." She looked pointedly at Ruth. "You too; She wants to see the both of you." The bedsheet slid down and exposed his well-defined chest as he sat upright. "Over my dead body," he said.

Stephanie appeared in the doorway. She looked amused, and it fueled his anger. He hissed as he bared his fangs, but she was undeterred. "You should be careful what you wish for Matthew," she said, "That last statement can easily be arranged."

In a blur, Matthew had his hand around her throat. Her eyes bulged as he squeezed, but she quickly regained her composure, grabbed hold of his wrist, and removed his hand from her neck.

"I would advise you to be mindful when you speak to me." She sneered, utterly unimpressed by his nakedness. "You're wrong about that," he scoffed. "When Isabella's bored with you, which in my opinion will be very soon, she'll toss you to the side, and you will no longer be under her protection." He smiled wickedly. "When that happens, it will be a free for all for anyone you've pissed off with your jumped-up pretences of being someone of importance." He looked her up and down with distaste. "Mark my words; your position beside Isabella is only temporary."

Ignoring his harsh comments, she turned and made for the doorway. "Get dressed," she said. "You know how Isabella hates to be kept waiting, especially when she's in a bad mood. I'll wait for you in the car."

Ruth handed him his trousers. "Take no notice of her," he said reassuringly, "she's a drama queen." He turned his back as he dressed. He didn't want them to see the worry on his face as the severity of their situation nestled heavily on his shoulders.

Scene Seventeen: Questioning

Standing just inside the huge greeting hall, Ruth turned in a circle in open admiration. Despite the tension twisting in her gut, she couldn't help but marvel at the broad open stairway that caressed the walls in a semi-circle in front of her. Ornate dark brown mahogany banisters stood out against the walls' brilliant whiteness, and luxurious, deeply colored carpets graced the stairs and floor. A large, tasteful sofa with highly polished mahogany tables sitting at each end filled the space along the wall to their left, and a large, white marble statue of a naked man with his arms stretched out to either side of him stood in the center of the room.

"Follow me." Stephanie barked. She escorted them through an archway to the right side of the hall, entered another large room, then pointed to several chairs lined up against one wall. "Wait here." She said.

One whole hour passed before a council member came to escort them to Isabella's office. "Hello Matthew," he said, offering his hand warmly in greeting. "Many a year has passed since we last met." The smile reached Matthew's eyes as he stepped forward and shook his old friend's hand. "Joseph, you old dog," he said affectionately, "How the hell are you?" "It saddens me to say, Matt, but I'm doing a lot better than you are at the moment. She's ready for you now, but please, watch your tongue; She's in a foul mood."

Ruth stepped forward and held out her hand. "Hi," she said, "I'm Ru..." He cut her off.

"I know who you are, young lady. It's nice to meet you." He pushed her hand aside and pulled her into a hug. "I only wish it were under different circumstances." "Let's get this over with then, shall we?" Matt said. "I can't stand all this drama."

He took Ruth's hand as Joseph led them down a long narrow corridor that led to Isabella's office and gently tapped on the door before entering. Isabella sat with her bottom neatly perched on the front of her desk. She looked stunning in a figure-hugging white dress showing ample cleavage. The white high-heel stiletto shoes on her feet took her to just over six foot, but the bun sitting on the top of her head gave the illusion that she was even taller.

Stephanie Mercer and Isaac Callahan, a senior member of the council, who, along with Stephanie, was not one of Matthew's greatest fans, stood to either side of her.

Ruth could easily understand why

Matthew would be mesmerized by Isabella's beauty, even without the use of her influence. Her jet-black hair wonderfully accentuated her pale skin, and her blue eyes, large and piercing, had a seductive look all of their own.

With her eyes focused directly onto Ruth's, Isabella spoke in a blunt, even tone. "And so we meet." She said. Ruth knew she was in the presence of someone with great power, and sensing her nervousness, Matthew squeezed her hand in a silent reminder that he was there with her.

"What's this about, Isabella?" Matthew interjected, "Why are we here?" Isabella completely ignored him; her eyes remained focused firmly on Ruth. "Are you mute, girl?" she asked in a more than threatening tone. Without warning, Ruth snapped. Anger raged through her body and fed her newfound courage the meal of a lifetime. "No, I am not." She bit back defiantly. Isaac Callahan raised an eyebrow at Ruth's apparent lack of respect for the mother of all but one, but no one was more surprised at Ruth's outburst than Matthew.

Isabella's eyes narrowed as her expression turned icy. The mouse she expected to see residing in the girl before her was nowhere to be seen. She stood from her desk, clasped her hands behind her back, and slowly walked towards Ruth. She hissed as she bared her fangs. "You would be wise to soften your tone with me, newborn." She glared, daring her to interrupt. "I will ask you this question once and once only. Did you kill your mother's attacker?"

Matthew squeezed her hand tighter in a silent warning to be respectful. "No. I did not," she said, "I give you my word." "Your word means nothing to me, girl." Isabella snapped. "But mine does, doesn't it?" Matt interrupted, "*I*, give you *my* word. Ruth had nothing to do with the death of that vile man." Isabella's unsettling gaze glided to Matthew's face as she stepped directly in front of him. "Silence." She barked. "You know as well as I do that we've had to clean up her mess before haven't we, Matthew. I warned you then about keeping her in line."

He didn't want to anger her but felt that he had no choice but to plead Ruth's innocence. "And since that time, she hasn't put a foot wrong, Isabella. I promise you. She's learned that that sort of behaviour will not be tolerated, no matter who you are."

To everyone's complete surprise, Isabella turned and walked back to her desk. "Fortunately for you," she said, "I *do* trust in your word Matthew, but you, of all people, know the rules. If I discover that she had a hand in the death of her mother's attacker or anyone else for that matter, then I personally, will stand over you and watch you destroy her, are we clear?" He nodded. "Perfectly."

She waved her hand in dismissal. "Leave now." Relieved, Matthew cleared his throat. "Will your driver take us home?" He asked, "Dawn is approaching." Isabella leaned forward and glared menacingly. "Then I suggest you run."

Scene Eighteen: Murder

Beth blew a kiss to her husband and disconnected the facetime call. "Dad's working late tonight," she said as Callie passed her in the hallway. "Are you off out?" she asked. Callie picked up her car keys from the small side table in the hallway and kissed her mother lightly on the cheek. "Yeah," she said, "Riley and I are going out for some food. See ya later, Les." She called out.

Lesley appeared behind her sister, and together, they watched Callie walk down the pathway and get into her car. Beth closed the front door and turned to her sister. "I'm gonna have a quick bath, and then we can watch a movie and eat chocolate until we're sick." She said. Lesley's eyes lit up. "It's a date." She said and walked into the kitchen to rifle through the larder for supplies. She took out two large family-sized bars of chocolate, a tub of popcorn, some cheese and onion crisps, and four cans of soda, then placed them on a tray by the kitchen window, but as she turned to leave the room, she saw movement in the back garden, so she opened the back door and stepped outside. In the blink of an eye, Jessica appeared right in front of her, and she quickly stumbled back into the house. "Be calm," Jessica commanded, "step outside and keep your fucking mouth shut."

Confused that she had no control over her actions, Lesley stepped barefoot onto the patio and stared at the strange girl standing in front of her in her sister's backyard. Jessica took her by the hand, dragged her to the side of the house, grabbed her by the throat, and pushed her up against the wall.

"Just so you know," she growled, "I'm a vampire, and I'm here to kill you; why? Because I can." She threw her head back and laughed. "I'm killing you because I want to inflict as much pain and misery as I possibly can on your fucking cocky daughter, who, by the way, is also a vampire, did you know that?"

Lesley's eyes opened wide with shock as the strange girl's words sank in. She cried in pain as Jessica grabbed her face and squeezed, then turned it to the side. Isabella had ordered that Lesley was to die with a smile on her face, so she licked the skin on her throat to numb the area and released her fang serum into her as she fed.

When Lesley was dead, she picked her up and carried her to a brightly coloured sunlounger and laid her onto it, then she bit into her wrist and allowed droplets of her blood to fall in and around Lesley's mouth, and smudged it to look like she had drank from someone.

She stood and ran her tongue over her fangs as she looked down at her victim and imagined Ruth finding her mother this way. "Isabella was right." She thought sadistically. "This is really gonna fuck with her head. She's gonna think that someone's gone and vamped her; Stupid fucking bitch." She took her mobile from her back pocket and snapped a photo so she could show off tonight's work to Isabella, spat on Lesley's body, then disappeared in a blur.

Scene Nineteen: Discovery

Beth wrapped a large towel around her body and a smaller one around her long thick hair. Leaning closer to the mirror, she puckered her lips together and ran her fingers over the fine lines that meandered from the corners of her eyes. She smiled as she remembered that her sister was downstairs waiting for her with a box of chocolates and a tub of salted popcorn. They hadn't spent any real quality time together for years, but tonight would be the start of rectifying that.

She unscrewed the top from her nighttime moisturizer and wondered if Lesley would like to use it too. She applied the cream to her face, dried herself, and put on the pyjamas she had set on a stool in the bathroom, then she combed through her wet hair, picked up the night cream, and took it downstairs with her.

"Les," she called as she walked into the Lounge. "Where are you?" She walked into the kitchen, but the lights were off, and the room was empty. "Les," she shouted again, "are you in the loo?" Still, the house remained silent. A growing sense of unease crept over her as she walked from room to room, looking for her sister, but she was nowhere to be seen. "Ahh, garden." She thought. "You'd better not be out here sucking on a cancer stick," she shouted jokingly. "You promised me you'd kick that disgusting habit."

She stepped out onto her beautifully maintained lawn and looked from side to side, then frowned when she saw Lesley lying on one of the sunbeds with her face turned away from her. "What are you doing out here?" she joked, "You won't get a tan this time of night." She was puzzled when there was no reaction and walked across the grass to her sister. "Les, I'm talking to you." She said, her voice awash with growing irritation.

Her breath caught in her throat when she reached her, though. There was blood around her mouth, and her sister looked back at her with dead blank eyes. She fell to her knees, and even though she already knew that it was too late, Beth shook her sister as if she was trying to wake her up from a deep sleep.

After a few agonizingly long moments, she dragged her sisters' body onto the grass, wiped some of the blood from her face with the sleeve of her pyjama top, and gave her mouth to mouth, but still, there was no response. She sat back on her heels and cried into her hands. After a few minutes, she gathered herself and went back into the house. Her hands trembled as she took her phone from her bag and dialled Ruth's number. "Hi, Beth," Ruth answered. For a long moment, she was greeted with nothing but her aunt sobbing.

"What's wrong, Beth?" she asked. Still sniffling, Beth started to talk. "Ruth. Get here quick," she said, "it's your mum." Panic raced through her entire body as she looked at Matt and Tori. "What's happened?" She asked. "Is she OK?" Beth continued to sob uncontrollably, and Ruth could barely make out what she was trying to say. "She's dead," she heard her aunt cry. The phone fell from Ruth's hands, and Matthew hastily picked it up from the floor and put it to his ear. "We're on our way Beth," he said solemnly, "Sit tight."

Beth went into the kitchen and splashed cold water onto her face and neck, then she picked up her phone and dialed Jack's number as she walked back out into the garden and sat next to her sister on the grass. She picked up Lesley's hand and held it as Jack answered the call. What Beth hadn't noticed were the bite marks on her sister's throat.

Scene Twenty: Heartbreak

Ruth raced into Beth's Garden, ran to where her aunt still sat, then fell to her knees. Her whole body shook as she held her mother's lifeless body to her chest and rocked back and forth. Matthew hugged Beth, then influenced her to be calm and to go to the front door and invite the woman who waited there to come into the house.

He turned and placed a comforting hand on Ruth's shoulder. "I'll take her inside," he said gently. "No," she said. "I will." Matthew followed closely behind Ruth as she lifted her mother, carried her into the house, and up the stairs to her bedroom, where she took great care as she gently laid her down on the bed. Inconsolable gut-wrenching sobs fell unabated from her as she dropped to her knees and laid across her mother's body.

Tori gasped as she entered the room and saw the blood around Lesley's mouth. She looked at her brother, and they shared a silent thought. Matthew gently moved the collar of Lesley's pyjama top aside with his finger. Bite marks. To all intents and purposes, it looked as though she had been parented, but by whom and why.

Ruth shook her head. "I don't understand," she sobbed, "she was doing so well. I spoke to her earlier on the phone, and she said that she felt a lot better. She had a hospital appointment this morning and said that they were so pleased with her progress that they were probably going to discharge her after her next appointment in a fortnight's time."

He took hold of Ruth's arm and gently pulled her to her feet. "I'm so sorry, darlin'," he said, "but her injuries have nothing to do with her death." He moved the collar of Lesley's pyjama top aside. Ruth's eyes opened wide when she saw the puncture wounds. "What the hell?" She cried.

All heads turned as the bedroom door opened, and Beth entered the room. "I can't believe this is happening," she cried, "I went to the hospital with her for her check-up this morning, and they said that she was healing nicely. The doctor was astounded when she told her that she had managed to stop drinking without any help and said that it was nothing short of a miracle." Fresh tears streamed down Ruth's face as she remembered being the one influencing her mother to kick her alcoholism to the kerb.

Beth crossed the room and looked down at her sister's body lying on the bed. "Do you think this could be from the lung that was punctured?" She gestured to the blood around Lesley's mouth but gasped when she noticed the bite marks. Suddenly, she felt as though she were on the set of a vampire movie. "What the hell's going on?" She said.

Matthew was glad that he had influenced her to be calm when he had first arrived at the house but knew then that he had to help her further. He smiled sadly as he stared into her eyes. "I'm so sorry, Beth," he whispered. "Don't be sad, and don't worry; All will be explained to you later. I promise. You should go downstairs and wait for Jack and Callie to get home; they're going to need you to look after them when they get here." She nodded and silently left the room.

Ruth felt as if she were in a dream. "I don't know what to say," she said, "why has this been done to her, and who would have done it?" She shook her head. "None of this makes any sense." "I know it's hard," Matthew inserted, "but try not to think about that for now." "How can she not, Matt?" Tori said nervously, "I think that this is a direct attack on us; It has to be. Indiscriminate parenting's frowned upon, and it's too much of a coincidence to..." Matthew shot her a glare. "That's not helping Tor," he said, "Ruth needs time to digest what's just happened. We can discuss it after we've had time to properly think it through."

Ruth smiled a silent thank you. "Did you say that it takes two days to transform Matt?" She asked. His heart broke for her. "Yes, darlin'," he said softly.

Ruth sat next to her mother on the bed and stroked her hair lovingly. "Is there anything I need to do for her?" she asked without taking her eyes from her mother's face. "When I parented you two," he said, "I washed your body and dressed you in my mother's nightgown, but I didn't do it because it needed to be done; I did it because I wanted you to feel comfortable as you slept, and to allow you to maintain your dignity."

Ruth stood from the bed and brushed a few blades of grass from the front of her jeans. "I want to do the same for her." She said. She felt numb as she walked over to her mother's chest of drawers and took out a beautiful pair of pink lace pyjamas. She held them up in front of her face. "She'll look pretty in these."

Scene Twenty-One: Parented?

Callie pulled her car onto the driveway and ran into the house. Fresh tears poured from Ruth when she heard her cousin cry downstairs, and Matthew told her that he would go and comfort her. She nodded in gratitude as he left the room but remained silent. She had hardly taken her eyes from her mother's face since she had washed her body and dressed her.

She turned, but only briefly as her cousin came into the room and sat on the floor next to the bed. Callie's eyes were bloodshot. "I asked Matt what happened, but he said I should speak to you," she said. "Why is she lying like this?" She gestured to Lesley's body. "It looks like she's been parented," Tori said from the corner of the room. Callie's eyebrows drew together in confusion. "What? Parented; How?" "I don't know," Ruth whispered, "but I promise you, I'm gonna find out."

Scene Twenty-Two: Suspicion

Matthew re-entered the room. "Ruth," he said, closing the door softly behind him, "She can't be here when she wakes up; We have to take her to my house." Ruth remembered her own awakening, and she gasped as the reality of what was happening hit her hard. "Of course we should," she said frantically, "and we need to figure out what we're gonna do about her first feed. Maybe we can find someone like Wayne Thomas." She cringed as she said his name. "Easier said than done." He thought but didn't voice it aloud. "Try not to worry," he said, "we have two days to figure something out." "I'll drive," Tori said as she left the room.

Matthew gently laid his hand on Ruth's shoulder. "I've told Beth and Jack everything," he said. "How did they take it?" She asked. "Well, I used my influence to help them," he said, "and I had Callie for back-up. She was a big help." He put his arms underneath Lesley's body and gently lifted her from the bed. "Let's get this done," he said.

He followed Ruth from the room and carefully carried her mother down the stairs. Tori had pulled the car as close to the house as she could. The last thing they needed was for a neighbour to see what was going on. Ruth got into the back seat, and he gently laid her mothers' body across her lap. Ruth sobbed as he got into the car, and Tori drove them home.

When they got there, Tori disappeared inside the house and was already waiting for them in the torture room with fresh linen when Ruth, followed by Matthew carrying Lesley's body, arrived in the basement. Ruth made up the bed in the alcove where she herself had previously slept in death, then stood back and beckoned for him to lay her mother on the clean, crisp white sheets. Her bloodshot eyes followed her mother's body as he lowered her onto the bed.

"Do you think Isabella had something to do with this?" She said, waving her hand over her mother, "maybe this is her way of getting back at me for taking you away from her because let's face it, Matt, she'll never be happy about us being together will she." "I don't think so," he said, "I mean, not only is it going against all of the rules of the council, but it's too obvious." Ruth shook her head, "how can you be so sure?" She watched him as he stood in silence, trying desperately to puzzle it through.

"No," he finally said, "I think this is someone who wants to stir up trouble between Isabella and us, and my money's on Stephanie." His voice was heavy with disgust.

"The more I think about it, the more convinced I am that she had a hand in it."

Ruth sighed and shook her head. "No, I don't think so," she said, "you told me that she's always tried to undermine your authority in the past, but at this moment in time, you're out of favour with Isabella, and she's right there beside her, so she's already got what she wants." Tori nodded. "I agree," she said, "think about it, Matt; Why would she risk her new position by doing something as serious as this behind Isabella's back?" Ruth's eyes opened wide. "Or she did it *with* Isabella's blessing, or even by her order."

Shock waves resonated through the room at Ruth's assumption. Matthew still found it hard to believe that Isabella would break her own rules in such a way, but what Ruth had just said made so much sense. And, was it possible that Isabella had also ordered Jerry Weller to be killed to cause a rift between him and Ruth? Whatever it was that was going on, the whole scenario stank, and he found it increasingly difficult to believe that Isabella was not involved in some way, but he decided not to voice his suspicions to Ruth for the time being; The last thing he needed was for her to do something out of anger, especially if he was wrong, so instead, he tried to play it down. Plus, he could be overthinking things, but he knew it was a long shot.

"We have to stay calm," he urged, "we can't accuse them of anything until we have solid evidence. Besides, and please don't take this the wrong way, darlin', but if Isabella is involved, she would have just killed your mum because she never parent's randomly. She once told me that you could count the amount of her children on one hand, and considering that she's thousands of years old, that's quite a bold statement. I seriously doubt that she would break her own rules just to make a point."

Ruth stayed quiet. She didn't know what to think but most definitely knew what she had to do.

"I need to get out of here," she said, walking over to the door. "I'm just gonna go back to Callie's and make sure that they're all alright. Look after her for me." "Of course I will," he said, "but please darlin'; Until we know what's going on, be careful." Ruth nodded solemnly, and in a blur, was gone.

Scene Twenty-Three: Confrontation

The last year of my life has been a fucking shit storm," she said as she stood in Matthew's Uno Parente's orangery, "so if you're gonna kill me, then can you just get it over with, and if not, can you please just answer my fucking question?" The last two words, she screamed.

Ruth didn't flinch as Isabella appeared right in front of her; Fangs bared. When she had said that she flat refused to live in fear, she meant it, and the anger at losing her mother had increased her resolve. "My my," Isabella said with a wry smile, "someone got out of the wrong side of her coffin this evening." Isabella glared at her guards. "Get out." She barked.

Eyes fixed straight ahead, Ruth shook with anger but stood dead still as Isabella slowly circled her. "You dare to come to my house and accuse me of what? Parenting your mother?" She said with distaste. "Personally, I can't think of anything that would make me want to "parent your mother." She air quoted.

Ruth glared as Isabella came to a halt in front of her, but the tears of anger she'd been holding back brimmed, then spilled from her eyes. Isabella hid her amusement; She was so enjoying her game of cat and mouse with this one.

"How dare you speak to me so disrespectfully." She said in warning. "Do I have to remind you that you're already walking on thin ice? I ought to kill you for suggesting such a thing. Still, fortunately for you, and out of respect for Matthew, I gave you the benefit of the doubt when you pled your innocence in the killing of Jeremy Weller, so do not test my patience any further by accusing me of parenting your mother."

Isabella returned to her seat. "Not that I have to explain myself to you," she said, "and Matthew should have told you this before allowing you to come here to see me this evening, but I never, ever, parent on a whim. I always select my children with great care, so believe me when I say this for the last time; There is nothing on this planet that would make me want to parent your mother."

Ruth's expression darkened. "Matthew doesn't even know I'm here," she said, "and he *did* tell me that you rarely parented, but I wanted to ask you myself so that I could see your face and would know if you were telling the truth."

Isabella bit back a smile as Ruth continued to rant. She had to admit; This girl had a sizeable pair of balls on her and was nothing how Jessica had described.

"If it wasn't you," Ruth continued, "then was it your fucking sidekick, Stephanie? Matthew told me that she has always hated him. Maybe she did it to piss you off and to cause trouble between us."

Isabella licked her lips as her eyes slowly traveled up and down the length of Ruth's body. She hated to admit it, but she liked her sass. It turned her on. Under different circumstances, she would have enjoyed taking her *and* Matthew to her bed. Still, maybe it wasn't too late. Perhaps she would influence them to indulge in a bit of menage a trois with her before introducing them to real death. She would see how she felt when the time came.

Ruth saw the lust in her eyes and scoffed. It annoyed Isabella, and her eyes narrowed as she leaned forward in her seat.

"Well, now that you're here, and I've graciously answered your question," she said, "I have something I wish to ask you in return. Apart from the fact that you're easy on the eye, tell me what it is that Matthew sees in you? Because from where I'm sitting, I find you extremely whiny and irritating."

Something deep inside Ruth snapped, and although she knew that her next words could bring her dangerously close to her real death, she was surprisingly unafraid. Her chin jutted out defiantly.

"Love, passion, humility, honour, forgiveness, empathy, and compassion. All the things that you clearly do not, and never will have. If I didn't dislike you so much, I would actually feel sorry for you, Isabella. You're surrounded by vampires who cater to your every whim. Fawning over you left, right and center, but let me tell you, they don't do it out of love or admiration; They do it because they're terrified of you. Yeah, sure, I don't doubt that many, if not all of your lovers, have said the words "I love you" during sex, but I'll bet that that's the only time they ever said it. The truth is, that you have never, in all of your existence, been truly loved by anyone.

Ruth's words touched a nerve. Isabella wanted more than anything to rip her throat out, but she held herself in check. She was glad that no one else bore witness to this conversation. They would be confused as to why she tolerated such insolence from this newborn, and their curiosity could lead them to discover her intentions and may even reach Matthew's ears, and she didn't want that. She and her accomplices had put too much time and effort into her plan for it to end with Ruth's death in this room tonight. Besides, she was so looking forward to watching Matthew's misery as he watched his whore die. She leaned forward in her seat

"If you find it easier to convince yourself that Matthew has never loved me, then that's your prerogative," she said, "but let me assure you that during our time together, Matthew loved me with all his heart and soul. I made him over two hundred years ago, and I know him inside and out." She smirked as she settled back into her chair. "You, my girl, are deluded if you think that you could ever be his one and only because that person doesn't exist and never will. OK, at this moment in time, you probably fit that space, but it won't last. Before long, he'll grow bored, and your pretty little face won't be enough to keep him. Matthew has always had many lovers, even when we were together, and if you don't believe me, then ask him yourself." Isabella's face wore a look of satisfaction as she continued. "It would take a lot more than you to keep him in a monogamous relationship because he craves not only sex but also chaos and violence; it's why he's such a good assassin."

Ruth knew she was just saying those things to hurt her. Matthew had told her that he had never in his entire life been in love with anyone but her, and she believed him. She balled her hands into fists and took a step closer. She was angry because she had come here to find out who had parented her mother, but somehow, Isabella had skillfully diverted the conversation onto Matthew. Her eyes narrowed, and she sneered as she spoke.

"I don't know why I'm wasting my time by asking you about my mother; when she wakes up, she'll tell me herself who did this to her, and if she decides not to transform, and dies for real, then believe me when I say, that I will never, ever, stop hunting until I find whoever did this to her, and when I do, I, will end them." She stood back, and in the blink of an eye, she was gone.

Scene Twenty-Four: Devastated

Rain began to fall as dawn approached. It felt cool on her face as she reached Sedan Street and entered the house. When she got inside, all was dead silent but for the gentle noise of the rain as it gathered in momentum and thudded against the windows. She felt a sense of unease as she made her way back down to the basement and couldn't shake the dread she felt in her chest.

As she entered the torture room, Matthew sped across the floor in a blur and blocked her view of her mother's body. He wrapped his arms around her. "I'm so sorry, Ruth," he said softly. "She's gone." Panic swelled in her chest. "What do you mean?" She cried. "She can't be gone."

She struggled to break free, but he held on to her tightly. "How do you know?" She sobbed into his chest, "It's only been a few hours, and you said that it takes two days." Matthew felt her pain. "Her body has stiffened," he said, "She has rigor mortis, so she must have decided not to transform."

Ruth's mind raced in a multitude of different directions as real grief burned deep inside her. Matthew thought that the decomposition of her mother's body was because she had decided not to complete her transformation, but it suddenly occurred to her that she could have been murdered. Tears streamed unabated from her eyes, and she wiped a trembling hand across her face. Again, she pushed away from him, and this time, he allowed it to happen.

"No. My mother wouldn't leave me," she cried. "Not now. Not after we reconciled, and she was on the road to recovery. No, Matt, I think someone did this for a cruel joke. I was fucking stupid and naive to think that she'd been parented," she said venomously, "I think that someone murdered her and staged it to look that way. I mean, come on, Matt, think about it, what possible reason would *any* vampire have to parent my mother? It's not as if parenting is an everyday occurrence, is it?" She shook her head at her own stupidity as she crossed the room and knelt beside her mother's body.

Matthew didn't have to be able to sense her emotions to know that this was killing her. He entwined his fingers at the back of his head and paced the floor.

"As soon as the sun sets, I'll talk to my eyes and ears on the street," he said, "then I'll go to the mansion and ask Isabella outright if she or anyone she knows is involved." "I've already done that," Ruth said without turning to look at him, "and she denies all knowledge of it."

Matthew's jaw hit the floor. He thought that maybe he hadn't heard right. "What do you mean?" he said. "I already asked her." She answered. "On my way back from Callie's, I found myself standing at the gates of her mansion, so I went inside and asked her myself."

Matthew was stunned but angry that she had again acted without first discussing her intentions with him and his sister. "What do you mean, you *found* yourself standing at the gates?" He scoffed, "you knew *exactly* what you were going to do. I thought it odd that you would want to leave the house and wondered if you might do something stupid, but I told myself that you wouldn't lie to me again; Not after what happened before."

Ruth looked up at him with bloodshot eyes. "You're right, Matt," she said, "and I'm sorry, but this is different. I needed to look her in the face and ask her myself if she or Stephanie were involved. Of course, she denied all knowledge of what had happened to my mother, but I don't believe her. I'm telling you, Matt; If it wasn't her, then she fucking knows who it was. Either way; She's involved."

She bent and kissed her mother's cold cheek. "I'll make her pay for this, mum." She promised as she stroked her face.

She stood and turned to face Matthew. "If she wants a fight, then I'm up for it." She said. "I know that I don't stand a chance in hell against her, but I have to try."

Matthew shook his head. "Stop jumping to conclusions, Ruth," he snapped, "There are a lot of disgruntled vampires out there who hate my guts and would love to see me meet my real death. I've assassinated a lot of vamps in my time, many of whom have had partners that have vowed to end me. It could be one of those."

"Stop it, Matt." She said. "You know as well as I do that something's going on. This isn't just going to go away. She's coming for us, and you know it." "I agree," Tori said from the corner of the room. As much as he wanted to diffuse the situation, he had had the same feeling in his gut since he had first been summoned to see her a few weeks previously. They had to fight. "OK," he said.

Ruth's eye's narrowed with cold contempt as she straightened her back. "OK," she said. "This is war."

Scene Twenty-Five: Approach

He stepped from the shadows and stood under the glow of the solar-powered streetlamp that burned outside the house and watched as Matthew, Ruth, and Tori appeared in the living room. Pulling his hat down further to hide his face, he walked onto the driveway and tapped gently on the front door, and within moments, he stood face to face with the man he'd come to see.

Matthew looked on edge. He instantly knew that this man was a vampire. "What do you want?" he asked bluntly. The man stepped backward and held up his hands in a friendly gesture. "There's no need for aggression, Matthew." He said in a deeply rich, velvety voice. "Please, may I enter?" He turned and scanned the street. "I have urgent business to discuss that concerns you, and there's a very real possibility that we're being watched."

Ignoring his request, Matthew stepped outside the house and pulled the door closed behind him. It wasn't necessary for a vampire to ask for permission to enter the home of another, so he knew he had asked purely as a measure of politeness. Still, this vampire was strong and had an air of authority about him, so he kept his guard up and was ready to fight in an instant.

His firm and well-defined, muscular, athletic build fit neatly into the beautifully tailored suit he wore. He stepped forward. "Let me introduce myself," he said. He held out his large, ham-fisted hand in greeting and smiled. "My name is Marcus Steroni."

Scene Twenty-Six: Reveal

Marcus thanked Tori as she handed him a glass of whiskey. He swirled it around in the glass before downing it with just one gulp. "Isabella has told me about you," Matthew said. "She told me that she destroyed your twin brother when he grew bored with his immortality and drank his way through an entire village full of innocent people."

The glass shattered onto Marcus's lap as he squeezed it. Several shards entered his hand, but the wounds healed soon after he pulled them free from his flesh.

"Yes, that's true," he said through gritted teeth, "but I bet she left out the part where it was *she* who told him to do it to ease his boredom." He said menacingly. "Anthony told her that he considered walking out into the sunlight, so she said that she would grant him this one discretion."

Matthew raised his eyebrows in clear disapproval. "Don't look at me like that," Marcus snapped, "we were Roman soldiers who had been raised with violence. You have absolutely no idea how hard we fought to keep our true nature in check. Every night was a struggle, especially for Anthony." Visibly restraining himself, he sat back in the chair and licked the blood from his fingers.

"I've spent a great deal of time and effort to bring about our beautiful but vile parente's destruction," he said, "and in recent years, my associates and I have made great progress." "It doesn't sound like you've achieved much of anything," Matthew scoffed, "only recently, Isabella told me of your threat but said that you hadn't made a single attempt to destroy her. In fact, she said that you hadn't been seen or heard from in eight hundred years."

Marcus pursed his lips angrily as he rose from his seat. "Don't be such an arrogant prick," he growled, "before you make comments like that, you should take a good look at yourself because your recent behaviour does nothing but to suggest that you've gone soft." Marcus looked Matthew up and down with contempt. "Word has it that you haven't slain a single unruly vamp in weeks because you've lost it," he said scathingly.

An awkward silence ensued. Marcus was right. He often thought to himself, and had even once mentioned it to Ruth, that since meeting and falling in love with her, he had neglected his duties as chief assassin, but the truth was that he had, in fact, stopped doing them altogether. What surprised him, though, was that word of his inactivity in the killing field had spread and was being widely discussed within the vampire community.

"You don't yet know to what extent, but you desperately need my help, Matthew, so you would be wise not to piss me off." Marcus continued. He stood, crossed the room, and peeked through the curtains. His eyes darted from side to side as he scanned the empty street. "I understand your mistrust, but I'm here to help you," he said, looking back into the room, "I promise you, we're on the same side. I want her gone as much as you do, perhaps even more. She took my twin, and if there's anyone who can understand the wrench I still feel from losing him, even to this day, It's you."

Matthew glanced over at his sister and nodded. "I do." He smiled softly. He couldn't bear the thought of the world without his sister in it. Tori smiled back, then addressed Marcus. "Please forgive my brother," she said, "not only is he deeply in love and very protective, but he's also under a lot of pressure at the moment, you see, we've had a very recent bereavement." Marcus nodded curtly. "I'm aware of what has happened," he said, looking at Ruth, "and I'm sorry for your loss," his gaze returned to Matthew, "but your attitude isn't helping the situation. I have put myself in grave danger by coming here to see you, and a little gratitude wouldn't go amiss. Now, do you want to hear what I have to say, or would you like me to leave? The choice is yours," he said.

Matthew nodded. "I apologize," he said, "but you're wrong if you think that I've lost it." Marcus arched an eyebrow. "I never said that I believed the rumors," he said, "your reputation as a hunter precedes you." Matthew acknowledged the compliment with a curt nod of his head. "Stay," he said, "and tell us how you already know about Ruth's mother."

Again, Marcus peered through the curtain before returning to his seat. "This may surprise you, but I have eyes and ears on the council, and one of them recently overheard a secret conversation between Isabella and her cohorts concerning the two of you."

Tension twisted in Matthews's gut. "Go on." He said. Marcus sat forward in his chair. "I'm sorry to be the bearer of bad news," he said, "but if you've ever planned for the worst-case scenario, then this is the time to action it. Isabella has secretly been orchestrating a plan to destroy you and who she refers to as your whore." Marcus softened his tone as he directed his gaze to Ruth. "I'm sorry to have to tell you," he said, "but it was she who ordered the killing of your mother. They deliberately staged it to look as if she had been parented to hurt you even further."

Unadulterated fury raged through her body. She could hear Matthew speaking to her, but white noise filled her ears. "I fucking knew it," she growled. "She has to pay."

Marcus cleared his throat. "I'm sorry, Ruth, but there's more," he said, "she also ordered the killing of your mother's attacker in the hope of coming between you and Matthew."

This confirmed his earlier suspicions. Divide and conquer. The oldest trick in the book. "Fucking bitch," Matthew said. He was ashamed to admit that her plan had almost worked because he had at first thought that Ruth's involvement in Jerry Weller's murder to be a genuine possibility, but now, he felt terrible for even thinking it.

"And I'm sorry, but there's more," Marcus continued, "as devastating as that is, it's not the worst of it. Are you aware that she has recently parented a young woman? My eyes and ears on the council say that at this time, she is a major player and is always by her side."

Matthew was puzzled by Marcus's concern. "Why is that such a problem?" He asked, "surely we've got a lot more to worry about than Isabella parenting another child." Marcus pursed his lips. "If only it were that simple," he said, "it's *who* she is that's the worry."

A sudden sense of dread swelled in Ruth's chest. "Who is it?" She asked. Marcus's voice was taut with tension. "Her name is Jessica Bartlett."

Scene Twenty-Seven: Fear

Ruth's head spun as shock flew around the room. "Are you sure, Marcus?" she asked, her voice shaking. He nodded solemnly. "You were being watched when you attacked her a few weeks back, and Isabella made it her business to track and parent her to use as a weapon against you."

Matthew shook his head. "You were right when you said that I'd lost it, Marcus," he said, "how could I have been so stupid as to think that she would let me off with just a warning when she found out about Ruth attacking Jessica? I've been such an idiot." "You've been distracted and off your game, but you're not an idiot." Marcus said, "You're only mistake was that you relied too much on her fondness for you, but she's a demon, Matthew; She couldn't love you if she tried, and don't forget, she's a master manipulator who's had thousands of years to hone her skills." Matthew nodded his gratitude.

Ruth remained surprisingly calm and looked directly at Marcus. "Will you help me kill her?" She asked through gritted teeth. He smiled as he nodded. "I will." He said. "You can't promise her that," Matthew inserted, "You of all people know how powerful she is, and not that she needs it, but she's surrounded by a multitude of faithful vampires who would go above and beyond to protect her. They would have no trouble ripping us to pieces."

Marcus smiled. "Oh, ye of little faith," he said, "I understand your concerns, Matthew, but believe me when I say that we are more than prepared for what is to come. Anyway, a good many of her "faithful circle of vampires" hate her, and have actually been working with me for centuries to bring about her demise. Believe me when I say that I have eyes and ears everywhere. On the council. Servants, and even some of the vampires that guard her. She is particularly loose-lipped around the latter." "But how do you know you can trust them?" Tori asked. Marcus's smile reached his eyes.

"Because they've proven their loyalty to our cause on numerous occasions. It has taken some of them centuries to embed themselves into her household and earn her trust, either as, like I said before, a servant, guard, lover, or advisor, and with their intel, we've been able to take a giant leap towards bringing about the end of Isabella's reign of terror," he answered, "the fact is, that together, we have already done far more damage to her than you could ever imagine."

"And that is?" Ruth asked from where she sat on the sofa. A huge grin spread across his face as he smiled proudly. "We have imprisoned her mother." He said.

Scene Twenty-Eight: Mother

Matthew's jaw hit the floor. "How can you have her mother when there's no one that I know of who even knows who she is?" He asked. "I was there when two of her council members asked that question, and they met an extremely violent end." "Yes, I heard about that," Marcus replied. "I discovered who she was by accident when she came to visit Isabella in Rome. My brother and I overheard them speaking as we approached Isabella's room. We didn't enter because the conversation was heated, and we could tell that Isabella was afraid. Can you believe that? Her voice trembled in fear."

Matthew couldn't believe what he was hearing. Isabella. Afraid. "What were they talking about?" He asked. "I don't know," Marcus answered, "They spoke in what I've since learned to be Adamic." Ruth sat forward in her seat. "Adamic? I've never heard of that." She said. Again, Marcus stood, walked to the window, and peered through the curtains, then turned and walked back to his chair. "Well apparently," he began, "it was the language God used to speak to Adam in the garden of Eden. It's often referred to as "The divine language," but who knows?"

Matthew sensed that Marcus was becoming increasingly unsettled, and he too crossed the room and peered through the curtains. Then, confident they weren't being watched, he returned to his seat next to Tori on the sofa.

"If they were speaking in a language that you didn't understand, then how do you know what they were arguing about?" He asked.

"Not all of the conversation was in Adamic," Marcus answered, "two words were repeatedly spoken in our native tongue. Latin." "And what words were they?" Matthew asked. Tension filled the room as Marcus stood and poured himself another drink. His hand trembled as he lifted the glass to his lips. "Mother, and Lillith."

The room seemed to seize with silence before Tori jumped from her seat. "Are you sure," she said, "You can't mean *the* Lillith." "I'm afraid I do," he replied. Matthew looked aghast. When he had been alive, he had heard his father speak that name on many occasions. It sent fear through his entire body.

Not fully understanding the severity of the situation, Ruth shrugged her shoulders. "Who's Lillith?" She asked.

Scene Twenty-Nine: Uncaring

Stephanie Mercer stood nervously in front

of the woman she loved and pleaded her case. "You can't trust her," she said, "she's a loose cannon, and you shouldn't be keeping her so close to you. I'm telling you, Isabella, there's something wrong with her. You saw what she did to her father. Even though he wasn't her favourite person in the world, he was still her father, and the extent of what she did to him was completely uncalled for, wouldn't you agree?"

In a blur, Isabella appeared directly in front of her and grabbed her by the throat. "You're telling me?" She growled. "Think before you speak to me as if I'm an imbecile."

Stephanie tried to explain that that wasn't what she meant, but Isabella tightened her grip in silent warning. "You've become very needy of late," she said through gritted teeth, "and not only is it boring, but it's becoming very, very irritating." She sneered as she looked Stephanie up and down with open distaste. "Granted, you have risen in the ranks because of the success you've had in your work with Matthew and his whore, but since I've taken you to my bed, you've gotten above your station. If you believe that you mean something to me, then you are sorely mistaken. You're just a tool I sometimes use for sexual gratification." Isabella smirked as she threw her to the floor. "I care nothing for you. Just stick to the task at hand and do as you have been told."

Matthew's recent harsh words echoed through her mind as she got back to her feet. "Now get out." Isabella ordered. Stephanie's heart shattered into a million pieces, and in the blink of an eye, she was gone.

Scene Thirty: Knowledge

Marcus's intelligent eyes shifted around the room. "Isabella isn't dead," he explained, "she was born a vampire. Her mother is Lilith, Adam's first wife, and she was cast from the garden of Eden when she considered herself to be Adam's equal. After she was expelled, she was so enraged that she mated with a powerful demon, Samael, and as a result of that union, the first-ever vampire was born; it was a daughter, and they named her Ishmalia, but for the last few centuries, she has used the name Isabella Marshond." Matthew was shocked to the core and couldn't believe that he hadn't put two and two together himself.

"Forgive me for asking," Tori said, "but how do you know all of this?" Marcus sat on the edge of the chair. "After hearing Isabella and Lillith's conversation, I had my suspicions, so after she murdered my brother, I scoured the earth for proof that I was right, and with the help of true scholars through the ages, I discovered an ancient scroll which confirmed my suspicions. Everything I just told you about Isabella's conception was written on it. I was then privileged to be introduced to some incredibly brave and powerful witches, who, by using magic from the light *and* the dark, have created a binding spell that is powerful enough to entomb even Lillith. She is presently being held in a cavern deep within the ground in Jerusalem."

"Did you know that Isabella has recently returned from Jerusalem?" Matthew asked. "Of course I did," he said, "as I told you earlier; Eyes and ears." Matthew noticed the gleam in his eyes.

Everyone tensed when they heard a knock on the front door. "Wait here," Matthew said as he left the room, but when he didn't return, Ruth went to see what was happening outside.

"What's going on?" she asked, but then she saw the body lying at Matthew's feet. This was too much, and she fell to her knees. "I know her," she said, "this is, or should I say was, Suzie Price, Jessica's best friend." Despite her newfound resolve, she didn't know how much more of this she could take, and tears filled her eyes.

"Go inside." Matthew said. In a blur, he bent and picked up the body and took it into the house before any of the neighbours saw what was happening. Suzie's body, curled into the fetal position, was frozen solid. It rocked a little as he gently laid her on the floorboards in the hallway. Her eyes were open wide; Frozen in a stare of death. He ran his fingers through his hair. "What the fuck." He said. "She's frozen solid."

The four vampires stood in confusion around the body. "She hasn't been parented, and there are no visible injuries that I can see," he said, "so what is this? What possible reason would they have to kill her and dump the body here like this?" Ruth's eyes never left Suzie's as she spoke. "Jessica doesn't need a reason for anything she does, Matt," she answered. "she does these things because she wants to. Her favourite pastime is violence; You of all people should know that."

Matthew looked uncomfortable. "I don't want to sound insensitive, but we have to get rid of the body," he said, "we can't leave her here. What if one of them calls the police and tells them that we have a dead girl in our house, and they come to investigate?" "I'll take it with me," Marcus said. "My people and I will leave her outside a police station."

Matthew noticed Tori's silence. "What's wrong, Tor?" He asked, "are you OK?" Tori's mouth was drawn into a tight line. She could no longer hold her anger in check. "No, I'm not OK, Matthew," she said. In a blur, she stood face to face with Ruth with her hands balled into fists.

"None of this would be happening if you'd done as we asked you before." She said. "*You* may have come onto Isabella's radar, but it's highly unlikely that your tormentor would have." She looked hard. All traces of the softness that usually surrounded her were gone. "This is all your fault, and if anything happens to my brother…" The rest of the threat hung in the air.

Ruth was shocked by her outburst but quickly recovered. "I don't need your permission to avenge my mother's death." She screamed. Tori moved closer. "Your insolent behaviour started before she killed your mother, so you can't use that as an excuse, and what happens when they come after the rest of your family because believe me, they will."

Ruth hid her surprise. Things had moved so fast in the last few hours that she hadn't even given Callie Beth, Jack, or Lizzie a thought. Her eyes narrowed as her temper rose. "Get out of my face Tor." She said through gritted teeth. You could cut the air with a knife as Matthew pulled them apart, and with his back to Ruth, he turned to face his sister. "Please, Tor," he begged, "even if Ruth hadn't attacked Jessica, I think that Isabella would still have come for us. I didn't mention it before, but when I went to my initial meeting with her, she wanted us to have sex. I declined as respectfully as I could, but it obviously made her angry. Please don't let this come between you. She's using the oldest trick in the book; Divide and conquer." Tori folded her arms across her chest and studied him for a moment. "You should have told us that before Matthew." She said.

Marcus broke the tension. "Ruth, gather your family together. We need to get them away from here because they won't be safe at home." He said. "Why," Ruth asked. "Surely, as long as they stay indoors, no vamp can get to them." "Of course they can," Marcus said. "All they need to do is knock on the front door, and when they answer it, all they have to do is use their influence to make them invite them inside, or they could throw a Molotov cocktail through the letterbox and burn them all to death or kill them as they run from the house. And also, don't forget, they have human helpers. They could just as easily get one of them, or come to think of it, any old

Tom Dick or Harry off the street to kill them. I'm sorry, Ruth, but Tori's right. They're far from safe."

Ruth was gutted. Her family was in this mess because of her. "What are we gonna do?" She asked, "we have to protect them." Marcus laid a reassuring hand on her shoulder. "Don't worry; we will," he said, "I have a property in Scotland where no-one will be able to find them. Get them here, and I'll make arrangements for my driver to pick you all up and take you to an airstrip where my private plane will be waiting. I still have a few things to do here, so I'll make my own way and join you at the house as soon as I can."

Ruth nodded in gratitude, then turned to Matthew. "Let's go and get them," she said, picking up his car keys. She disappeared into the lounge, took her mobile from her bag, and switched it on. When the screen lit up, she noticed that she had an unread text message from Lizzie. "Hello sweetheart," it read, "I wanted to cheer you up, so I've bought you a lovely present. Why don't you pop round and pick it up? XX."

Despite the mood, a slight smile appeared on Ruth's face. The kindness of this wonderful woman would never cease to amaze her, but then reality hit her like a bomb. "Lizzie," she said, "I can't believe I never considered her in all of this. She'll be just as big a target as my family, if not more. Jessica hated her almost as much as she hated me."

In a panic, she tapped Lizzie's number and put the mobile to her ear, but the call went straight into answerphone. Ruth realised that Lizzie had absolutely no knowledge that her mother was dead, or even that she and Matthew were vampires.

"Must have a flat battery," she said hopefully, more to herself than to anyone else. Preferring not to leave a voicemail, she disconnected the call and fired off a quick text message. "Hi Lizzie," it read, "Matt and I are on our way around to your house. See you soon, XX." Then, she highlighted Callie's number and handed the phone to Tori. "I want to get to them as quickly as possible, so would you mind calling Callie and telling her everything that's happened?" She asked, "tell her about going to Scotland and to get ready as quickly as possible because we're on our way to pick them up. Tori didn't relish the task but knew that time was of the essence. "Will do," she said.

Ruth started for the door with Matthew following close behind her when she suddenly stopped dead in her tracks. Her whole body shook as she broke down and cried. "What about my mum?" She sobbed. "We can't just leave her here. We have to take her somewhere safe until we figure out what to do." "Don't worry." Marcus said softly, "I'll make sure she's taken good care of." He took his mobile phone from his jacket pocket, pressed a number from his contacts, and put it to his ear. "I have a very dear friend who owns his own funeral business. I'll have him come over right away." He reached out and squeezed her arm softly. "He's a good man, Ruth, and I promise that he will take good care of her for you." She dried her tears on her sleeve, then placing her hand on his arm, she stood on her toes and kissed him lightly on his cheek. "Thank you, Marcus."

Scene Thirty-One: Disappointment

Stephanie stood stiffly at the foot of the bed where Isabella lay entwined in passion with her new pet, but this time, she stopped what she was doing and gave Stephanie her full attention. "And?" She asked with more than a tinge of impatience, "out with it. What happened when they saw the body?"

Stephanie, numb with heartbreak, gave her report. "Not a lot, really," she said. "Unfortunately, it was Matthew and his sister who came to the door. Ruth was nowhere to be seen." She lied. The last thing she wanted, was to satisfy Jessica's ego by telling them that she had seen Ruth fall to her knees when she saw Suzie's body, nor did she tell them that she had seen another powerful vampire enter their home earlier in the evening. "Matthew just picked it up and took it inside."

Jessica growled with disappointment. "Oh, for fuck's sake," she said, "this is getting fucking boring now Bella, You should have just let me take that stinking carcass round to them instead of her." She sneered as she looked Stephanie up and down with distaste. "It would have been fucking brilliant to see the look on Ruth's face when she saw me all fanged up. She would have shit herself." She exposed her teeth, hissed, then giggled.

Stephanie lowered her head and raised an eyebrow. "Bella?" She thought. She was shocked beyond belief that not only did Isabella not berate Jessica when she laughed, but she joked with her.

"Funny, my child," she purred, "but watch your tongue." Isabella's eye's narrowed in mock warning to her lover, "we don't want them to know that you are mine just yet, do we. The whore already suspects that I had a hand in her mother's death but is completely unaware of *your* involvement." Isabella's eyebrows drew together as she pondered the situation. "But you do have a point, though," she admitted, "we don't want them to go into hiding, so we'll action our plan in just a day or two, anyway, why so much impatience, my child? You had fun with the old one, did you not?" A cold hard smile covered Jessica's face. "Yeah, I really fucking enjoyed killing that dried-up old cow." "You're not supposed to drink them dry." Isabella scolded, but her new child grinned wickedly. "Sorry, mummy," she said in mock sarcasm, "but if it's any consolation, her blood tasted like cat's piss."

Their attention was drawn to the young man sitting in the corner of the room as a sob escaped his throat. "What are you fucking crying for?" Jessica sneered. "Are you jealous of my new girlfriend?" She ran her finger seductively along the skin between Isabella's breasts. "No," he stammered. "I'm…"

In a blur, Jessica appeared in front of him and grabbed his testicles. "Ahh," she cooed, "do these saggy things need emptying, Jase? Maybe you should go a few rounds with her over there, or ain't you that desperate yet?" She nodded towards where Stephanie stood. Stephanie sped across the room and wrapped her hands around her throat. "Get your fucking hands off of me you stupid bitch," she barked. She tried to remove Stephanie's hands from her throat but wasn't yet strong enough.

Amused at the spectacle, Isabella giggled. "Now now ladies," she said, "There's no need to fight. Stephanie, be a good girl and let her go. You should take this thing," she gestured to Jason, cowering on the floor, "to your room, and give him a good seeing to, especially since you haven't had any yourself lately." She added cruelly.

Stephanie, trying to retain at least a little of her dignity, declined Isabella's offer. "No, thank you," she said curtly. Her eyes darted toward her rival. "Unlike others in this room," "I still have work to do." A single tear dropped to her face as she turned and left the room.

Scene Thirty-Two: Struggling

Callie, Beth, Jack, and boy-boy were ready and waiting for them as Ruth and Matthew pulled up in front of their house. They quickly got into the car, and Matthew began the journey back to his house on Sedan street.

Beth sniffled from the back seat, and Ruth reached over and squeezed her hand. "I can't believe this is happening," Beth cried. "One minute, we're a happy family. I get my sister back, but she's brutally ripped away from me, and then, I find out that not only did *you* die as well Ruth, but you're a bloody Vampire! Someone, please wake me up from this nightmare; This can't really be happening."

Ruth was gutted. "I'm so sorry, Beth," she said. "I wish I could tell you that this was really all just a nightmare, but it isn't. It's real, and we have to get you to somewhere safe."

Tori appeared at the front door as Matthew pulled onto the driveway. He left the engine running as he got out of the car, took their suitcases from the boot, and led them inside the house. "Sit tight while we go and get Lizzie," Ruth said, "and if anything happens, do whatever Tori tells you to do, OK?" She looked at them expectantly as they nodded in assent.

Matthew smiled, trying to lighten the mood. "hopefully, we won't be too long," he said, then took Tori's arm and led her across the room. "Can you help them with your influence," he said in a low voice. "They're trying to be brave, but they're struggling." Tori smiled kindly. "Of course I will." She turned and approached Ruth's family. "Would you mind gathering around me folks," she said. "I'm going to give you a little help."

Scene Thirty-Three: Present

Even though the night air was hot and muggy, Ruth shivered as Matthew stopped the car in front of Lizzie's front door. She tensed when she noticed that it was slightly ajar, and the house was in complete darkness.

"Wait here," Matthew said. Ignoring him, she got out of the car and walked towards the house as Matthew pushed the door open a few inches wider, and they peered down the hallway. The door creaked as Matthew pushed it fully open, and they stepped into the house. "Lizzie," she called, "It's Ruth and Matt. Are you home?" They were answered with silence, so they continued on into the kitchen at the back of the house and switched on the light.

White LED lights lit the room, and a huge square cardboard box with a large bow and greetings tag tied around it sat in the middle of the floor.

"I don't like the look of this," Matthew said from behind her. She stepped forward and read the greetings tag. "For Ruthie," it read. The hair on the back of her neck stood up. Lizzie had never once called her that; the only person who had was Jessica. Her hands shook as she pulled the ties on the ribbon, and the bow came undone. She teased the end of the sellotape holding the flaps together and pulled it back. Her eyes opened wide with horror, and she screamed as Lizzie's empty eye sockets looked back at her from a face that had been beaten to a pulp. She had been stripped and tortured. Her knees were pulled to her chest, and her wrists had been bound with a thick, coarse rope. She had a gag in her mouth, and there were deep, what seemed to be cigarette burn marks pocketed all around her face and arms.

It was too much for her, and she fell back onto the floor, but Matthew pulled her to her feet and wrapped his arms around her. "I looked her in the eye, Matt, and promised her that she had nothing to worry about," she sobbed into his chest, "I promised to protect her, but look what's happened." She pushed away from him and stared at what was left of Lizzie's face. "Oh God, how she must have suffered," she cried, "they must have killed her and sent me that message from her phone," she sobbed, "I let her down, Matt, and now she's gone." She remembered that her mother was dead too, and her cries grew increasingly desperate.

"We have to get out of here," he said. "What about Lizzie?" Ruth asked, "we can't just leave her here, Matt." "I'm sorry, darlin', but we have to," he replied, "I'll stop on the way home and use a phone box to call the police. We'll leave the door open for them to come in and find her, but I'm sorry; We have to get back and protect the rest of your family." She knew he was right.

She stood and looked down at her friend through wet eyes. "I'm so sorry, Lizzie," she cried, "none of this would have happened if you hadn't tried to help me." Matthew growled. "None of this is your fault, Ruth," he said, "let's lay the blame for this where it truly belongs….Isabella."

Scene Thirty-Four: Safety

The moon was high in the sky as they pulled up to Marcus' safehouse in Scotland. The building consisting of three levels, was huge and square in shape. The walls on the middle floor were made entirely of specialist glass that blotted out the sun's harmful rays, making it safe for a vampire to look through them. Marcus smiled as he opened the front door and stood in the entryway. A thunderstorm had delayed their flight for long enough for him to beat them here by motorbike.

"How was your journey?" He asked as they entered the house. "Stressful, but comfortable, thanks to you," Tori answered, smiling. He stood back and gestured towards the living room. "Please," he said, "make yourselves at home."

When they were all seated, Marcus offered his hand to Jack. "I'm Marcus Steroni," he smiled. Jack took his hand and shook it warmly. "Thank you for this," he said. Marcus waved away his comment. "You're very welcome," he said, "I'm just so sorry that you've been dragged into all of this. You and your family are just innocent bystanders and don't deserve to be caught up in this mess. It's not fair that you have had to uproot your family, but I give you my word that my associates and I will do our utmost to destroy the vampires responsible." "I know, but thank you all the same," Jack replied. "Can I take the dog out for a walk? He's still a little jumpy after flying for the first time," He added.

All heads turned as the lounge door opened, and a woman appeared in the doorway and spoke. The voice came from a slightly built but toned woman as she entered the room and flashed a good, clean, sincere smile. "Hi everyone, I'm Anna. If you would like to follow me, I'll show you all to your rooms," she said, "then, when you've settled in, we'll meet back here, and you can tell me what you would like to eat. You've had a long and stressful night; You must be starving." The woman's casual demeanor did wonders for Marcus' guests, and all but Ruth and Matthew followed her down a long, brightly lit hallway and disappeared around a corner that led to the guest bedrooms.

Marcus stood before Ruth and took both her hands in his. "I'm sorry to hear about what they did to your friend," he said. "That only shows you how vile they are, doesn't it? But take heart to the fact that you are not alone. There are hundreds of vampires who are working tirelessly towards Ishmalia's demise." His eyes glanced sideways and landed on Matthew. "Thank you," she said, "I think I'm gonna need all the help I can get." "Well, at least you won't have to worry about the safety of your family," he said, "my team has created false identities and have made arrangements for them to live here for the rest of their lives if the unthinkable happens, and we lose the fight. Money won't be of any concern for them either as I've put a substantial amount into a new account for them, and they will have around-the-clock protection if their covers are blown in the future. Ruth stepped forward and threw her arms around his neck. "I don't know how to thank you," she said.

Marcus hugged her back, then gestured for them to sit on the sofa. "Now, let's get down to business," he said. He directed his gaze to Ruth. "Do you know how to fight?" he asked. Embarrassed, Ruth momentarily looked down at her feet, but when she looked up, cold hard determination covered her face. "I think it's fair to say that I couldn't fight my way out of a paper bag if my life depended on it, but I want to learn because *I* want to be the one who kills Jessica," she said, jabbing her finger angrily into her chest. The shock of finding out that her tormentor was now a vampire and was now in close cahoots with Matthew's Uno

Parente, had worn off, and she was ready for war. "Because of her, my mother and Lizzie are dead, and so am I. Her best friend Suzie has lost her life, and even though he deserved it, that piece of shit Jerry Weller is dead too."

"Marcus pursed his lips. "Good, because I think you can safely say that not only your life but that of your entire family, not to mention Matthew and Tori is at stake." His eyes slid onto Matthew. "Perhaps you can indulge Ruth with some of your legendary fighting prowess." He said. Matthew smiled. "Definitely."

Marcus clapped his hands and rubbed them briskly together. "OK," he said, "it won't be long before they realize that you have gone into hiding and will think you have done so because you're running scared, so they won't be expecting us to bring the fight to them. I think we should stay here for as long as necessary. As of yet, they're still unaware of my presence, so we can use that to our advantage." "How can you be sure that they don't know about you being on the scene?" Matthew interrupted, "we can't just go on summarization." "Were not," Marcus replied, "My eyes and ears on the council have said that there's been no mention of my name and are confident that Isabella is completely unaware that I'm even still alive, let alone in the vicinity and plotting her downfall." Matthew wasn't convinced. "Who on the council are you referring to?" He asked, "give me some names."

Marcus paused before answering. He had no other option but to trust them. "Suffice it to say that you must never utter the names I'm about to divulge to you outside of this room." Matthew nodded assertively. "Of course." He said.

"Maybe this won't come as a surprise, but Joseph Abrams is one among them. He tells me that you and he are old friends." Matthew's smile reached his eyes. "No, you're right," he said, "I'm not at all surprised that Joseph's working with you. He's a good man."

"Yes, he is." Marcus agreed. "He's a good man, who's witnessed Isabella at her worst, and has grown to hate her with a passion. He has wanted out for many years now, but as you already know, once Isabella has her claws in you, that's where you will stay for the rest of your existence or until she grows tired of you."

Matthew nodded in understanding. "Who else is with you?" He asked. "We are a mixed bunch," Marcus replied, "some of us are warriors, while others are scholars, but we are privileged to have several members of the council on our side. They are Freida Meyer, George Wadman, Severin Slovak, Mary Brunyee, Terence Cox, Ella Taylor, Peter Halsey, and this one may surprise you, Isaac Callahan. Matthew's jaw hit the floor. He had always firmly believed that Isaac was devoutly loyal to Isabella.

"Right now, you could knock me over with a feather," he said, exasperated, "he's never hidden the fact that he dislikes me a great deal; I've always thought it was because he thought I was below Isabella." Marcus grinned. "No, he just thinks that your status was above what it should've been. He always refers to you as the upstart." Marcus bit back a smile. Matthew knew that Isaac wasn't the only council member who felt this way. "I'd call that jealousy." He said indignantly but then broke into a genuine smile. "Mary Brunyee," he said. "I love that woman."

All heads turned as the lounge door cracked open a few inches, and Anna Sommers peeked into the room. Her intelligent, bright, sharp eyes scanned their faces, then finally settled on Ruth. She smiled, then stepped inside. "Would you like to come and freshen up?" she asked with a warm smile. She had a way about her that, although they looked very different, she reminded Matthew of Maggie Lawley, a lovely woman from his youth who had been the housekeeper to his best friend, Jeremiah Tundy, and his wife Sarah, and who he had eventually helped to pass away peacefully when she contracted consumption. He smiled fondly at the memory of her.

Ruth stood and brushed imaginary fluff from the front of her jeans. "Thank you so much," she said. Marcus nodded as they passed him and left the room.

As they walked along the hallway, Anna turned and spoke over her shoulder. "Do you guys need to feed?" she asked, "Some of Marcus' family of donators live here with us and have already offered their services to you." Both Ruth and Matthew shook their heads. "No, we've recently fed," Ruth said, "but thank you anyway." "Tori said the same thing," she said, "but as soon as you feel the urge, let me know, and I'll make it happen." Matthew saw the twinkle in her eyes, and again, he thought fondly about Maggie Lawley.

She stopped in front of a larger-than-average wooden door. Strange etchings had been carved deep into the wood, and Matthew ran his fingers over them. "What are these?"

he asked. "Spells," she said without hesitation. "No one, not vampire or human, can enter this room without your permission. Even Isabella herself has no power over you when you're inside. All you have to do is to lay your hands on the symbols on the wood and recite these words, but because there's two of you, you both have to say them together." She handed Ruth a piece of paper with an incantation written on it, and she held it up so that Matthew could read it also. "By the power and protection of the beloved and just Hecate," they said in unison, "we, upon entering this room, have sole authority as to who may enter this sanctuary. No-one will have sway or influence over our thoughts, emotions, or decisions, and no-one can harm us, be they dead or alive until we leave this place of our own volition." To their astonishment, as if an invisible hand had maneuvered the handle, it turned and clicked as the door opened.

Anna remained where she was as they stepped inside the room. "Shall we see if it worked?" she asked. As she tried to step over the threshold, the room filled with a noise that reminded Ruth of being underwater, and a wall of what looked like a thick, see-through membrane covered the entryway and prevented her from entering. She looked up and smiled. "I think we have our answer, don't you?" she said.

Ruth was agog. She was only just getting used to the fact that vampires existed, but now magic as well!

Anna nodded passed them. "Your bags are already in the room. I'll leave you to settle in.

Scene Thirty-Five: Sorry

Callie curled into a ball and sobbed as she laid on the bed. No matter how hard she tried, she couldn't stop reliving the heartache of her last conversation with Riley when he had told her that he loved her. He had stayed quiet after saying it, waiting for her to say that she loved him back, but she had remained silent.

Her heart shattered as he broke the silence and begged her not to leave, and she died inside at the thought of never seeing him again. She had to stay strong, though; Isabella and her lackeys had murdered her aunt and

Lizzie, and Matt and Marcus had said that it was only a matter of time before they came for her and her parents as well, so there was no way she could have stayed. She loved him more than anything, but his life would be in constant danger if she took him with her to Scotland, so the only thing to do, was to let him go.

She sat up, pulled an already damp tissue from under her sleeve, and dabbed her eyes. Unfortunately, because they had left at such short notice, she had had to tell him that she was leaving over the phone. She had said that her work as an assistant to the head project manager for a large building company was taking her to Ireland to oversee the refurbishment of a large estate that was way behind schedule, and that she would be gone for six months at the very least.

She would never forget the heartbreak in his voice when she had said no to his offer to drop everything and travel with her. Her sobs grew louder as she remembered when she also told him that it would be ok for him to date other people while she was away because she would be doing the same in Ireland. She didn't want to sound so cold and hated saying things that she knew would hurt him, but knew it was the only way that he would let her go.

A short series of beeps announced that she had a new text message, and she pulled her mobile from her bag. Her heart skipped a beat when she saw Riley's handsome face smiling back up at her from the screen, and a fresh wave of tears flowed freely from her eyes as she read it. "Please come back, Cal," it said, "I love you." Callie couldn't believe that even after everything she had said to him, he still wanted to be with her. She felt that love or happiness would never touch her life again.

Scene Thirty-Six: Gutted

Flickering light from the TV bounced from the walls in the darkened room as Riley James lounged in his oversized armchair. Images flashed across the screen, but he had no interest in them. Callie had left and had turned him down when he had asked to go with her. He texted her that he loved her, but she ignored it, and he was absolutely gutted.

He thought that things were going really well and had even toyed with the idea of asking her to move in with him soon, but now, she was gone, and he couldn't understand what had happened. Concerned for his well-being, Debbie had called him earlier when he hadn't turned up for work this morning but quickly became irritated when he told her that he just didn't feel like it today.

At twenty-six years old, Riley lived alone. His parents had died in a car crash when he was fourteen, and until he was twenty, he had gone to live with his aunt Rose, who was a good friend of his now boss, Debbie.

His stomach growled, and he realised that it was ten o'clock in the evening, and he hadn't eaten yet. He walked into the kitchen, opened the fridge door, and took out a beer, then reached into his food cupboard for a tin of baked beans. He opened the cutlery drawer, picked up a fork, closed the drawer with his hip, pulled back the ring tab, and ate them cold, straight from the tin.

Scene Thirty-Seven: Unremorseful

Sitting naked on the edge of Isabella's bed, Jessica Bartlett rocked back and forth with excitement as her Uno Parente spoke the words she'd been waiting to hear. "The time has come to reveal ourselves." She said, "Matthew and his whore have had time to work out what's been going on around them, and they must not be allowed to flee." She threw a withering glare at Stephanie. "Send a dozen assassins to Sedan street, and tell them to bring them here...Alive."

Sitting on the floor across the room, Jason Hardwick pulled his knees to his chest and cried. Jessica rolled her eyes then looked at him menacingly. "Do you know what you smell like, Jase?" In a blur, she stood before him. "Dinner." She growled. She pulled him up by his tee-shirt, dug her fingernails to either side of his windpipe, and yanked it from his body. His hand flew to his throat in a desperate attempt to stop the flow of blood as he fell to his knees, then flopped onto his back, and coughed and gagged on his own blood.

Grinning cruelly, Jessica towered over him. She filled her mouth with saliva and spat it onto him as his legs kicked out, and he thrashed around wildly on the floor. "You've been next to fucking useless." She screamed. "The only fucking thing you've come in handy for lately is your fucking chest freezer. What happened to you?" She mocked. "You used to be cool man."

His eyes glazed over as he passed away, but she felt no remorse for him or for what he had once meant to her. Jessica smiled and closed her eyes. Dying was the best thing that had ever happened to her. She couldn't wait to reveal herself to Ruth and vowed to make her pay for what had happened in the alleyway that night. No one had ever treated her that way before, so she wasn't used to being on the receiving end, but she was going to make damn sure that it never happened again.

Stephanie stood in shock. She couldn't believe that Isabella was allowing her new pet to behave in this manner. If anyone else had killed a human in front of her like that, she would have ended them on the spot.

Isabella glowered at her. "Stephanie," she barked, "what are you gawping at? Send out the assassins."

Scene Thirty-Eight: Fury

Isabella was beyond angry when her assassins had returned empty-handed from Sedan Street. She stood from her chair as Joseph Abrams entered the room. "Find Matthew Welsh and his whore." She said through gritted teeth. "My eyes and ears have informed me that they have been on a killing spree and have fled to who knows where."

He raised an eyebrow, and she threw him with a withering glare. "Do you dare to question what I've just told you?" She said through gritted teeth. "I have trusted intel that they have recently killed several innocent families and pinned the blame on an innocent man by planting evidence in his house. Now, that poor man is missing, so they must have silenced him with death." She stared at him, daring him to interrupt, but he stayed quiet. "I know that Matthew is responsible," she continued, "but most of the blame lies with the whore. Matthew was a highly respected member of my council until she arrived on the scene."

Joseph knew the truth about these murders, and that Wayne Thomas, the "innocent man" that Isabella had just mentioned, was anything but innocent, but he played along.

"As a council member, you will be aware that my mother and I created this institution to hunt and destroy any vampire who kills humans at random," she continued, "and now it turns out that my chief executioner has gone off the rails, but even he is not immune to my wrath, and if he thinks he is, then he is about to discover that he is sorely mistaken."

Joseph knew he had to be convincing. "To be honest with you, Isabella," he said, "I'm not surprised to hear this. Matthew has been different since he chose to parent again. I have found him to be offensive of late, which is quite out of character for him, so I agree with you. I think he has been greatly influenced by his new child. Don't worry; I will find them and bring them to you." He said.

Isabella looked almost maniacal as she sat back in her seat. "Make sure you do, Joseph," she said venomously, "find Victoria and torture her if she doesn't reveal their whereabouts. Anyone, even her, who is found to be aiding and abetting them, will meet with the same fate as they do, now get out of my sight."

Scene Thirty-Nine: Pride

Matthew beamed with pride. Considering that when she was alive, Ruth's temperament had been a soft and gentle one, but as she had trained with him, she had morphed into a more than half-decent fighter. The first week had been used to learn the art of self defence, but the past three were purely dedicated to the art of killing. His eyes travelled the length of her body. She was truly amazing.

Most people who had gone through what she had, would have been reduced to a blubbering heap, but Ruth was all business; Inspired and driven with the passion for avenging her mother and Lizzie's death, she had blossomed.

She held her fists tight to her face and bounced on the balls of her feet as they sparred. Matthew expertly moved his head aside as she threw a right jab, then quickly followed with a left. "I'm gonna enjoy killing that bitch," she sneered as she circled around him.

Matthew dropped his guard and stepped back out of arm's reach. "Let's call it a day," he said, pulling the sparring gloves from his hands, "Marcus' family of donators have kindly offered to feed us, and I want to grab a shower first." He wiggled his eyebrows suggestively, "Want to join me?" He put his arms around her, but she wriggled out of his embrace and slapped his arm playfully. "No, you go ahead," she said. "I want to carry on for a bit. We're going back tomorrow, so I want to be ready."

She crossed the room and took up her stance at the punchbag. "Be careful not to hit it too h..." Matthew called, but it was too late. Plasterwork fell to the floor as the bolt holding the chain to the punchbag was ripped from its placement. Her eyes gaped as she stood back and marvelled at her strength. "Oh no," she said. "I got a bit carried away. Marcus will be pissed off at me." Matthew laughed as he shook his head and left the gym.

Scene Forty: Promise

Beth, Jack, and Callie walked the four vampires to the front door. Ruth opened it, stepped outside, then turned and threw her arms around her cousin. Callie fought back the tears that threatened to fall from her eyes. Through no fault of her own, her life had fallen apart. Although she stood before her, her cousin had died, and so had her aunt, and now to top it all off, she had lost Riley, the man she knew she would have spent the rest of her life with.

She took a deep breath to calm herself; The last thing Ruth and the other vamps needed was her blubbering all over them. "I wish you didn't have to go," she said, "I should have just let you kill her in the alleyway that night." Ruth tried to make light of the situation and smiled. "It wouldn't have changed anything,

Cal," she said, "we would still be in this mess. There's no way that Isabella would ever have let us live in peace, and Jessica would still have done what she did."

Beth stepped forward. Not being able to cope as well as her husband and daughter, her eyes were rimmed in dark red circles through lack of sleep and unrelenting stress. "Make sure you kill her to death, Ruth." She said, "make her suffer for everything she has ever done. But whatever happens, promise me that you'll all come back home." Ruth smiled as Jack put his arms around his wife and pulled her to him. "We will, Beth," she said. She looked over her shoulder at Matthew and the others. "We promise."

Ruth bent and gave boy-boy one last scratch behind his ears, then turned and walked to the car waiting to take them to the airstrip.

Scene Forty-One: Anger

Over the past two thousand years, Marcus Steroni had fought hard against his thirst for violence and had eventually mastered the art of restraint, but now, he shook with anger. "You've done what?" He said, "this could jeopardize everything we've worked for over the past few hundred years, Joe. How could you be so bloody stupid?" He dragged his hand roughly over his bald head as he paced the floor. "If you're wrong about this, then it's over; you know that don't you. Everything we've done, every chance we've taken, and more importantly, every vampire that sacrificed their lives to get the information we needed will all have been for nothing," he continued, "because if Isabella finds out about us, our deaths will be anything but quick and painless. She would keep and torture us for centuries." Joseph opened his mouth to speak, but Marcus cut him off.

Joseph Abrams glanced around the room not only at Ruth, Matthew, Tori, and the other council members who were with them, but also four assassins led by Jane Strudwick. "I know," he said, "so please believe me when I say that I would never have taken the chance if I were not one hundred percent certain that she would join us. I've been watching her closely from the inside for some time now and have been witness to her demise within the ranks of Isabella's confidents." "Who is it?" Matthew asked. Without raising his voice, Joseph spoke. "Come in." He said.

To everyone's surprise, the door opened, and Stephanie Mercer entered the room. Before he could stop himself, Matthew laughed out loud, then shook his head in disbelief. "Oh, hell, no." He screamed. "Are you fucking mad, Joe?" Stephanie cleared her throat. "Please just hear me out." She said, stepping forward and closing the door behind her.

"Is this a joke?" Marcus asked angrily. In a blur, Peter Halsey had Joseph's throat in his hand. "We should kill you for this betrayal." He seethed. Terence Cox appeared at his side. "Let him go, Pete," he said. "If he hadn't approached her, then I would have. I, too, have been watching her reactions to the way Isabella allows the new dog to behave and agree with Joseph." He paused and focused his gaze on Ruth. "I honestly believe that she wants to see the dog dead just as much as you do, if not more." Ruth bared her fangs. "I seriously fucking doubt that," she growled.

"You do realise that the dog is only a by-product of our main mission, don't you?" The voice came from Ella Taylor, a slender wisp of a woman. She stepped in front of Stephanie. "Our main target is to destroy Isabella. Is that what you truly want?"

Stephanie's body trembled with emotion.

"All I can say is that I've been a fool." She said. "I have done everything for Isabella, and it still wasn't enough." "I told you this would happen," Matthew smirked, a little too happily for Stephanie's liking. "I know you did." She bit back. "but you don't have to ram it home," she said, "as long as she exists, I will suffer, so I want her gone. She doesn't want me, so if I can't have her, then nobody can."

"Ahh, diddums." Matthew rubbed imaginary tears from his eyes with his knuckles. "I don't trust you," he said. "You're gonna have to do a lot better than that to convince me that Joe was right to recruit you." Stephanie paused and closed her eyes. "I honestly don't know how to do that," she said, "but what I can do is to tell you everything that has happened so far." "That's fucking obvious," Matthew said through gritted teeth. "We already know what's happened." He leaned forward, "Do better." He growled.

Stephanie nodded. "I can be your eyes and ears," she said, "I will report everything they say and plan, to you, so you will always be one step ahead of them." She looked at the other council members. "Isabella didn't confide in a single one of you of her intentions to kill Ruth, and Matthew did she. Only Jessica and I know about it, so it's not as if you will be of any use on the inside as eyes and ears because, as far as she's aware, none of you know what her true intentions are. You've just been told to hunt them down for killing humans. She hasn't told you the real reason why she wants them." She paused and locked her eyes onto Matthew's. "Just think of the advantages of having me on the inside," she paused for emphasis, "you need me." Stephanie straightened her back as she waited for them to respond. She meant every word she said. Isabella had treated her appallingly, and she had had enough.

"Well, what's done is done," Peter said, "there's no turning back now. We have to decide to either kill her or trust her to work with us." Marcus glared. "Jane, would you mind taking her to the cellar while we discuss what to do with her? I don't want to take the chance of her bolting." Senior assassin Jane Strudwick gave a curt nod, opened the door, and escorted Stephanie from the room.

Scene Forty-Two: Test

Council members stood dead still as Isabella raged in a fury. Plaster fell from the huge crack in the wall when she grabbed the legs of her desk and tossed it across the room, where it smashed into pieces and scattered across the floor. In a blur, she decapitated several of her guards with the dagger she held in her hands, and their bodies crumbled into dust.

Isabella ambled slowly along the line her council members had formed and paused in front of Joseph Abrams. "I ordered you to find them, but still, they are nowhere to be seen," she growled. "Where are they?" Joseph cleared his throat. "I'm sorry, Isabella, but after searching extensively, we have been unable to discover their whereabouts." He glanced at each of the council members who stood to either side of him. "We have all had our eyes and ears searching but to no avail. It's as if they've dropped off the face of the earth." He spoke to an empty space as Isabella appeared in front of Stephanie with her fangs bared. "Do you have anything to add?" She demanded.

This was the moment of truth, and Joseph, Isaac, George, Frieda, Terence. Peter and Ella fought hard to keep the fear from their faces. They were about to find out if deciding to trust Stephanie was the right thing to do. Relief swelled through each and every one of them as Stephanie answered. "No," she said, "the assassins we sent said that there were no clues as to where they had gone. Do you think that there's a possibility that they found out that you knew about their killing spree and walked into the sun?" She asked. Isabella closed her eyes in thought. She seriously doubted it, but she wouldn't blame them if they had done just that. What she had planned for them was dastardly, even for her, but if that were the case, then it would mean that she had tolerated Jessica and her tantrums for nothing.

She glanced over to where Jessica sat looking smug, and for a brief instant, she considered ending her there and then, but two things saved her from destruction. One, just like Matthew, she excelled at sex. Isabella had had thousands of lovers, and very few came even remotely close to satisfying her as well as she did, and two, she wanted to watch Matthew's despair when she made him watch as Jessica killed his whore. The thought of watching him would make it all worthwhile, so instead, she beckoned her forward. "Everyone else; Get out." She ordered.

Scene Forty-Three: Meeting

Ruth and Matthew held hands as they sat next to Tori on the sofa in Marcus' London apartment, where they were staying as his guests, but when the living room door opened, Matthew flew from his seat in a blur and threw his arms around a beautiful, petite woman as she entered the room.

Mary Brunyee had been with Matthew through some tough times and had saved his life on several occasions when he first became an assassin. She was one of the bravest people he had ever known, and he loved and respected her with all his heart and soul.

"Hi stranger," he said as he picked her up

and spun her around. She grinned from ear to ear as she wrapped her arms around his neck and squeezed tightly. "Darling," she giggled, "how the hell are you? I hear you've fallen in love; She must be something else." Her hand flew to her mouth, "or is it a he?" She teased. He mock-glared as Tori joined them and hugged Mary for all she was worth.

"I've missed you," Tori said, "where have you been?" Mary winked, "working with Marcus," she answered, "we've been out of the country for a few years now, but I won't bore you with the details; Anyway, you're about to find out what we've been up to in a few minutes." Matthew knew a brush-off when he heard one, so he took her hand and led her to where Ruth sat. "Mary," he said, smiling, "it gives me great pleasure to introduce you to the love of my life. Ruth Myers."

The smile reached Mary's eyes as she grabbed Ruth's hand, then pulled her up from the sofa and kissed her cheek. "I know we'll become great friends," she said, "anyone who wins this one's heart must have supernatural abilities, I mean, apart from the ones we all have as vampires," she giggled.

Ruth instantly knew that she would grow to love this woman. There was an air about her that made Ruth feel more comfortable than she had done in a long, long time. It would have been wonderful if it were Mary who had parented Matthew instead of Isabella.

The room began to fill with council members, assassins, and several other vampires that were unknown to Matthew and Tori. "Please make yourself comfortable," Marcus said, entering the room. Matthew noticed Tori's eyes light up when he came in, and he bit back a smile.

Marcus rubbed his hands together briskly. "Well, from what I've been told, the meeting with Isabella was not fun," he said jovially. "But it proves we've got her rattled." "And I think it also proves my loyalty to you," Stephanie inserted from the back of the room.

Her eyes scanned their faces and finally landed on Matthew's. He nodded curtly, begrudgingly acknowledging her usefulness, and she nodded back in acceptance.

A female at the back of the room cleared her throat. "Pardon me for raining on this parade," she said, "this is all well and good, but the time for backslapping is nowhere in sight. How the hell are we going to kill her, Marcus? And is that even possible? I know you have her mother imprisoned at a secret location, but how is that going to help us?"

Lines appeared at the corner of his eyes as he smiled. "Yes, she can be killed." He said. "Just like us, she is vulnerable to sunlight, decapitation, and a stake through the heart." "That's what Seth Ahmed thought," Isaac interrupted. "Have you not heard of what happened when he put a stake through her heart? I was there, and I tell you, it was terrifying. He told no one of his plans to end her, and no one actually knows why he did it, but without warning, he just plunged it into her chest at one of the council's meetings. She just looked up at him and smiled as she pulled it from her body." "What happened to Seth?" Tori asked. Isaac shook his head with a hint of sadness. "Hidden somewhere and being tortured every minute of every day. Word has it that she has crucified him."

They gasped collectively. "When this is over, we will make it a priority to find him and end his suffering," Marcus said, "after all, it sounds like he's a kindred spirit. Why did he try to kill her?" "No one knows," Isaac said. "He took that secret with him to the torture chamber."

"So that leaves sunlight or decapitation," Matthew said. "Not that she needs them, but guards constantly surround her, and you've got no chance of getting her to walk out into the sun, so we're screwed." Shoulders slumped as Matthew's words sank in.

"I told you once before, Matthew," Marcus said. "You should never underestimate me. All eyes moved across the room. "I'm telling you, a stake will do the job." "But I've just told you; A stake won't work," Isaac said, full of frustration. "It will if it's made from the wood from the crucifixion cross." Marcus smiled as the room fell silent.

He inclined his head towards George Wadman. "Because of the unwavering bravery of this great warrior, we were able to discover the whereabouts of a sacred scroll that not only revealed this information, but also where to find the preserved and holy wood, so he, Mary Brunyee, and I were able to retrieve it, and I'm proud to say that it is now in our possession."

Everyone gasped, and it made Marcus smile. He looked around the room. "I promise you; We will be well-armed," he continued, "as well as the large number of deadly stakes we now have, Mary had the brilliant idea of incorporating fragments of the holy wood into arrowheads." The mood in the room had changed from one of gloom to one of growing confidence. "Even if Isabella is aware of what the holy wood could do to her, I'm fairly certain that she knows nothing of the scrolls' existence, so the fact that someone could kill her in that way has probably never even entered her head," George added.

"The scroll also revealed some other important information." Mary inserted, "as we all know, if a vampire drinks another vampire, it weakens them because the blood is dead, but anyone who drinks Isabella's blood will inherit powers that will almost match hers, so if there's a chance that anyone could do that, then" She smiled and shrugged her shoulders.

Ruth cleared her throat. "I'm sorry to interrupt," she said, "I know that destroying Isabella is paramount, but ending Jessica is equally as important to me. I want to fight and kill her first." Stephanie smiled. "I second that," she said. "Ruth, you and I should discuss how we can get her away from Isabella and to where you want the fight to take place." Ruth nodded slowly as she smiled. "Definitely."

Scene Forty-Four: Relief

Stephanie couldn't believe their luck when she and George Wadman bumped into Jessica in the hallway leading to Isabella's bedroom. "Jessica, we've been looking all over for you," she said. "Isabella wants you to try your hand as an assassin, so George and I are to escort you to a location in Kent to investigate a possible nest that's wreaking havoc there. She wants it shut down before it gets out of hand and reaches the tabloids." "But I was on my way back for another session," Jessica said, "she told me to come straight back after feeding on one of her donors. She's really gagging for it today, even more than usual, but you wouldn't know anything about that, would you."

Stephanie stepped forward to slap her, but

George quickly grabbed ahold of her hand and pulled her back. Completely unimpressed by Jessica's cruelty, he scowled as he shook his head. He had had to deal with the likes of her on numerous occasions when he had worked the door of some of the roughest pubs in London. "Grow the fuck up." He growled.

Stephanie was grateful to him for de-escalating the situation. If she had have hit her, it would have ruined their plans for the fight with Ruth. She ground her teeth. "Well," she said, "if you want to piss her off, then go ahead, be my guest, but I wouldn't want to be in your shoes when she finds out you've disobeyed an order." Her body trembled inwardly as she stepped aside and gestured for Jessica to pass. If Jessica called her bluff and carried on to Isabella's room, then she had either five minutes left to live, or would have to endure an eternity of pain.

Jessica thought about it, then grinned. "So, she wants me to train as an assassin. I've only been a vamp for five minutes, and I'm already ranked above you. Come on then: let's get this over with." George rolled his eyes, but Stephanie smiled as Jessica pushed past her, and made for the door.

Scene Forty-Five: Trap

They drove for just over an hour, then George pulled the car to a halt in a darkened lay-by about a mile away from the old disused storage facility that Ruth had chosen for the fight. He killed the engine, and they got out.

"It's down the road a bit," Stephanie said, "can you see those huge storage containers?" Jessica squinted her eyes and focused on the abandoned industrial site. "Our intel tells us that that's where they've set up camp and are holding quite a few humans that are slowly being drank dry. Now, as you know, Isabella and her mother created this organization in order to stop this type of behaviour, and you should consider yourself to be truly privileged for the honour of being chosen as one of their elite assassins, so follow my lead."

Jessica grinned. "I'm not surprised she chose me," she said, "I'm the bollocks, and it won't be long before the both of you are deferring to me cos I'll be your superior."

Stephanie fought hard to hide her loathing as George gently laid his hand on her arm in a silent warning to hold herself together. "Well, now's your chance to prove it," she growled, "let's go."

She couldn't wait to see this bitch get her comeuppance. She just hoped that Ruth was up to the job of killing her, but either way, she took solace in knowing that there was no way that Jessica Bartlett was leaving here tonight as anything but a cloud of dust."

Scene Forty-Six: Fight

Despite the warm evening breeze, Ruth shivered in anticipation and excitement. The air was full of tension as she turned and looked around the storage yard, and for the tiniest of moments, the thought that she may never leave this place crossed her mind, but there was no turning back now, even if she wanted to.

She reached into her back pocket and wrapped her hand around the hilt of the dagger she had brought with her, and she smiled. Since training with Matthew, her fighting skills had grown way beyond all expectations, and she had become a half-decent fighter.

Her hair blew around her face in the gentle breeze, and she pulled it back from her eyes as she looked up and smiled to where Matthew and Marcus watched from the shadows. She allowed herself a brief moment to think of a world without Jessica or Isabella in it, but her fantasy was only fleeting as Jessica suddenly leaped from the roof of a storage container and landed a few meters in front of her. She straightened her back and squared her shoulders. Her eyes showed her resolve; Not only was she was ready for this, but she was also going to enjoy it.

Matthew flicked the switch on the portable lights they had brought with them, and piercing white brightness lit the area. Jessica held her hands to her eyes in an attempt to shield them from the bright lights. When her sight adjusted, she stood with her hands on her hips.

"Oh, I see what this is," she said, looking back over her shoulder to where George and Stephanie still stood high above her on one of the larger containers. "Well, well, well. Who'd have thought you would have the balls. I wonder what Bella will have to say about this?" she said.

She turned back around to face Ruth. "I hope you know that I'm gonna kick the shit out of you. What happened in the alley outside Charlie's wasn't a fair fight, but now I've been gifted by Bella and have powers to match yours, so you're fucked."

Ruth was agog. "What?" she said, "are you stupid? Isabella never "gifted" you; She only changed you to use as a weapon against me. And what the hell would you know about a fair fight?" "Of course I'm not fucking stupid," Jessica retorted, "I know exactly why she chose me. She fucking hates your boyfriend, but to be honest, I've seen him, and I wouldn't mind squeezing his balls. Bella told me he can go for hours."

Ruth shook her head with disgust. "Very classy," she said, "I bet your parents are so proud of you." Jessica casually shrugged her shoulders. "Well, my mum is, but I wouldn't know about my dad," she said, "I ate him a few weeks back, didn't I Steph?" She looked back over her shoulder, but Stephanie was gone. She and George had joined Matthew and Marcus in the shadows.

Jessica turned back around and looked Ruth up and down. "Where are your manners?" She asked. "I leave you a beautiful gift; I even go out of my way to wrap it up in a pretty bow, and what? No thank you? How fucking rude."

Ruth took a step closer to Jessica, who stood with her arms, folded neatly across her chest.

"I think you're a coward," she said, her voice full of venom. "As I told you once before, you only pick the fights you know you can win. What chance did Lizzie have against a piece of shit like you? And what about Suzie? I'm assuming you had a hand in her death as well. What did you do to her?" Jessica rolled her eyes. "Pfft," she said, "what a fucking waste of time she was. All I did was show her my beautiful new fangs, and she goes and has a fucking heart attack and dies right in front of me and Jason, and oh yeah, while we're talking about him, he's dead as well; He was getting on my fucking nerves, so I ate him."

Ruth's eyes traveled up and down the length of her adversary's body with sheer and utter disgust. She had never imagined that anyone could be this vile and was eager to kill her, but there was something important she wanted to know first.

"Tell me," she asked, "I know it was you who murdered my mother, but was it your intention to kill her, or did you try to parent her?" Jessica sent her a scathing look of disgust. "Are you taking the fucking piss?" She asked. "Why the fuck would I want to parent that dirty whore?" she nodded her head with distaste. "Yeah," she said, "that's right. We heard about what she's been up to. Dirty fucking bitch. No. I didn't go there to parent her, but me and Bella thought it would be funny if you thought she had been. We imagined you sitting by her side, crying, holding her hand, and waiting for her to wake up. It was fucking hilarious, and I've got to tell you, we laughed our tits off."

Ruth was incensed. Her rage demanded immediate violence. In a blur, she grabbed hold of Jessica and screamed maniacally as she threw her across the yard. There was a loud crash as her body slammed into one of the shipping containers and left a massive dent where she landed. Before she had a chance to recover, Ruth picked her up and threw her onto her back. She straddled her and pinned her arms to the floor with her legs. Barely pausing between punches, Ruth's fists slammed into her face as she hissed and snarled as Jessica's head bounced from side to side as she struck her.

A vision of Lesley appeared in her mind, and for a fraction of a millisecond, Ruth hesitated. Jessica used that pause to her advantage. She raised her knees and threw Ruth off to the side before pulling a vicious-looking hunting knife from her back pocket and slicing it deeply across Ruth's throat, cutting deep enough to sever her windpipe. Ruth's hand flew to her neck as she instinctively tried to hold the significant slash together. She gagged on her own blood as she got to her feet, ran into the shadows, and dropped heavily to her knees, trying to stall for a few moments to give herself a chance to heal. Her hands remained over the wound, and after a few seconds, the flow of blood stopped, and the injury welded itself back together as if it had never even happened.

Marcus laid his hand on Matthew's arm when he felt him move. "Leave her," he whispered, "she needs to do this herself, and from what I've seen during your training sessions, is quite capable of beating her; besides, I wouldn't want to be in your shoes when you take the pleasure of avenging her mother away from her. Just give it a few more minutes." Matthew balled his hands into fists as he watched the woman he loved fight for her life and for justice.

Jessica jumped onto Ruth's back, but she threw her over her shoulder as Matthew had taught her, and again, she landed on the floor. Ruth stood dead still as she watched her nemesis get to her feet and brush the dirt from her clothes; then, she sauntered forward and stopped just in front of Ruth. Jessica smiled as she ran her tongue along her fangs. "My, my," she said, "someone's been practicing."

Ruth remembered the dream she'd had while she was going through her transformation, and her face broke into a genuine smile. In a blur, she thrust her arm out, and just as had happened in her dream, her fingers easily penetrated through the wall of Jessica's chest. She curled her fingers tightly around Jessica's dead heart, and pulling her forward, she whispered in her ear. "This is for my mum, Lizzie, and everyone else you have ever hurt." Jessica's eyes opened wide in shock as Ruth gritted her teeth and ripped her heart from her chest, then, showing no emotion, stood back and watched as Jessica's body toppled forward and crumbled into nothing before it hit the floor. Wearing a glove of her victim's blood, Ruth looked down at her hand as Jessica's heart did the same. Sneering, she casually rubbed her hands together and grinned as the blood moistened dust formed small sphere-shaped balls between her fingers.

George raised an amused eyebrow. "I've never seen that done before," he said. Matthew grinned from ear to ear. "What can I say," he said proudly, "my girl's resourceful, plus, she learned from the best," he added.
In a blur, Matthew, Marcus, George, and Stephanie surrounded her. She looked at each of them in turn and noticed the look of relief on their faces. Especially Stephanie's.

"One down and one to go," she said. George cleared his throat. "Sorry to run out on your moment of victory," he said, then turned to Stephanie, "but we should get back to the mansion. Dust girl said that Isabella told her to go straight back to her room after feeding, so she'll be wondering where she is by now."

"Ruth's face broke into a genuine smile. "That's OK," she said lifting her hands in front of her face, "I need to get out of here and wash this shit off of me anyway."

Scene Forty-Seven: Convincing

"Well, where is she?" Isabella demanded as Stephanie entered the orangery. An image of Jessica exploding into dust flashed through her mind, and she smiled inwardly.

"All I can tell you is what I said before, Isabella," she answered, "when I saw her leaving the mansion and asked her where she was going, she told me to mind my own business; You know what she's like; She hates my guts." Isabella grinned. "She hates everyone's guts," she said.

Stephanie's stomach churned as Isabella paced the room. "Something feels off," Isabella said, "I told her to come straight back to my room after feeding, but she never did. I haven't given her any tasks to do and certainly did not sanction her leaving the mansion, so, for her own sake, I sincerely hope that she hasn't taken it upon herself to do anything that would jeopardize our plans."

Stephanie shook her head. "Surely not," she said, "I know she's a bit unpredictable, but she knows how important it is for you to watch her kill Welsh's whore. Anytime now, she'll come back with her tail between her legs and throw herself at your mercy because she went out and fed on a non-consenting human instead of one of your donators.

Isabella shook her head. "No," she said, "I've already questioned my donators, and they told me that she fed on them. I'm telling you, something doesn't feel right. I can smell it." Her eyes narrowed as she threw a hawk-like gaze at Stephanie. "Have you done something to her?" She asked, "I know how much you hate her for taking your place in my bed."

Stephanie quickly realised that she was in a dangerous situation and had to be convincing. "No," she pled, "I won't deny that I hate her with every fibre of my being and would love nothing more than to see her gone, but I would never allow my hatred to get in the way of what we're about to do to your ungrateful child and his whore; As much as I hate to admit it, Isabella, she's far too important to the plan."

Not entirely convinced, Isabella stayed quiet as she considered her words. Stephanie had been a loyal and devoted member of her household for many centuries and had never given her any reason not to trust her, but still, there was always a first time for everything."

An uncomfortable silence told Stephanie that she wasn't out of the woods yet, and she had to fight hard to hide her terror. If she couldn't convince Isabella that she hadn't hurt her new brat, then she thought it highly likely that Isabella would introduce her to real death right here in this room, so she made her lip tremble and put on the best performance of her life as she crossed the room and gently placed her hand on Isabella's face.

"Please don't look at me that way, Isabella," she pleaded, "I have always loved you more than life itself and you know that. I would never betray you in such a way." "Well, if it wasn't you," Isabella said, "then Matthew and the whore must have eyes and ears on the inside; someone who is feeding them with knowledge?"

"But how can that be?" Stephanie said with a slight shake of her head, "only you, Jessica, and I know about what we have done; besides, Welsh doesn't have the balls to do something like that; in fact, I wouldn't be surprised if we never saw or heard from him ever again."

Isabella considered her words, then her face softened. "Come to bed," she said. "I have an itch to scratch." Genuine tears gathered behind Stephanie's eyes. "Nothing would please me more, Isabella," she said, "but I've made arrangements with senior assassin Jane Strudwick to pay a visit to the nightclub Jessica was at when I first saw her being attacked by Matthew's whore. She told me that she's frequented that place on numerous occasions and knows many of its regulars. She's even seen Jessica there in the past, so she can ask if anyone has seen her lately." Ignoring her words, Isabella placed her hand between Stephanie's legs and rubbed her gently. "That can wait." She purred.

Joseph Abrams knocked, then entered Isabella's office without waiting for her permission. "Isabella," he said excitedly, "I'm sorry to just barge in on you like this, but I have something of great importance to tell you. You're not going to believe this, but Marcus Steroni came to my home."

Isabella's eyes narrowed as she coldly pushed Stephanie away from her like a discarded piece of meat, and in a blur, she stood face to face with her council member. Her eyes narrowed in suspicion, but more than anything, she was surprised to hear of Marcus's return.

"Ah," she said, "so the proverbial coward has dared to show his fangs again, has he? Tell me, Joseph, why has he returned, and what does he want?" She asked.

Joseph knew he had to keep his nerve. If Isabella had even the slightest suspicion that he was lying, she would use her power to influence him, and if that happened, it would have dire consequences not only for him, but also for the cause.

He cleared his throat. Well, I'm afraid he came with bad news, Isabella," he said, "I'm sorry to have to tell you that your new child has been murdered."

Isabella threw a quick "I told you that something wasn't right," look at Stephanie. "Pffft," she scoffed, returning her attention back to Joseph, "is that all he has? Killing Jessica doesn't quite live up to his threat to kill me for ending his twin eight hundred years ago does it. He should know better than to think that losing her would hurt me, even if she was my child."

She shook her head in disappointment at Marcus's apparent lack of imagination and wondered how he had managed to become so soft and pathetic in his time away from her.

"If that's the best he can do," she continued, "then he is found wanting, so tell him that he needs to do better because killing Jessica is nothing more than an inconvenience to me."

Joseph did his best to look perplexed. "I don't understand, Isabella," he asked, "why is it only an inconvenience? She was your child." She waved her hand to silence him, and he eagerly complied. "Nothing that concerns you," she said bluntly.

Joseph shook his head and apologized. "I'm sorry for not explaining things properly to you, Isabella, but it wasn't Marcus who killed Jessica; It was Matthew and his child."

Her eyes narrowed. Instead of fleeing like she thought they would after killing the whore's mother and friend, they must have gone into hiding and plotted their revenge. "Ballsy," she thought. Again, she shot Stephanie another "I told you something wasn't right" look." She turned back to her council member. "Go on," she barked.

Joseph cleared his throat. "He told me that he heard on the grapevine that you had parented Jessica." "On the grapevine?" She interrupted, "Hmm, very interesting, continue."

Joseph nodded. "He said that he wanted to know more about who you had chosen and was watching outside in his car when he saw her leave the mansion unsupervised earlier, so he followed her and witnessed her being murdered by Welsh and his child."

"Why did he not help her?" She asked. "I asked him that very same question, and he told me that it was over before he realised what was happening, but Isabella, he was able to do something to make up for failing to save her and dare I say, that you might even consider it worth losing Jessica for."

Thoroughly unimpressed, Isabella threw him a withering glare. "This had better be good," she growled. Joseph forced himself to smile. "Oh it is," he said, "he said that he was able to take Matthew and Ruth as prisoners and is prepared to hand them over to you in the hope that you will forgive him for his past indiscretions because he desperately wants to be back by your side."

The air grew tense as Isabella fully digested this news. She had wanted to watch as Jessica killed Matthew's whore, but it wasn't the end of the world. Isabella's tolerance of her was at its end. Still, it was a shame that she was gone so soon. She was a skilled lover and would be hard to replace in her bed.

Intrigued, Isabella nodded curtly, "Tell me, Joseph, why did he come to you?" She asked suspiciously.

Joseph shrugged his shoulders. "I don't know why he chose to approach me," he said, "I suppose it's because we once worked closely together on council business, and I'm a familiar face."

Isabella looked thoughtful. "What else did he say, and where is he now?" she asked through gritted teeth.

Joseph shook his head. "I asked him, but he flat refused to tell me where he is residing. All he would say is that he wants to meet with you, but not here. He said that there's a disused shopping outlet in Essex that would be suitable, but stipulated that the meeting will have to take place during the day because he would feel safer if there was daylight between you. "Hmm, he thinks he's clever," she thought, "but if he only knew."

"Agreed." She said. "Get word to him that I agree to his terms. Tell him I've missed him; He was always one of my favourites."

Joseph smiled inwardly at the magnificent performance he had just given and praised himself in his thoughts. "And the Oscar goes to …"

Scene Forty-Eight: Connection

Marcus and Tori stood outside in the darkness. He couldn't help but smile as he looked at her out of the corner of his eyes. He thought she was beautiful. He had had countless sexual encounters with women from all walks of life during his existence, but with Tori, he felt a deep connection and hoped that she felt it too. It would be nice just to have that special someone in his life. Someone he could laugh with. Someone he could hold, who would hold him back and tell him that everything was going to be ok when he felt down, but most importantly, someone to love.

Tori interrupted his thoughts. "Obviously, the council will still need to be in place, so all we have to do is find someone who doesn't have psychopathic tendencies to run it." She looked at him and smiled. "What? Me," he asked, feigning surprise. "Yes, you, silly," she giggled.

Marcus nodded. "yeah, I must admit that I have given it some thought, but there are plenty of others who would do just as good a job at the helm as I would." "Such as?" She asked, "you're two thousand years old, Marc; there can't be many vamps who would have as much experience as you do." "Oh, you'd be surprised," he said, "There are plenty of others who are far older than I am, but they generally want nothing to do with vampire politics, so usually keep to themselves. We'll have to wait and see," he said, "don't forget that we have to kill her first."

Tori looked thoughtful. "Yeah, I know," she said, "but I still think that it doesn't hurt to look ahead. We need to be ready."

She ran her hand along his arm, and he shivered. The smile reached his eyes as he picked up her hand and kissed it. "Tori," he began, but she cut him off. She stood on her tiptoes and kissed him on the mouth. "Hmm," he growled passionately, "shall we go to my room?" She nodded, and in the blink of an eye, they were gone.

Scene Forty-Nine: Love

Soft candlelight flickered around the room he and Ruth shared in Marcus' luxury apartment. Matthew sat on a chair by the side of the bed and watched as the love of his life slept peacefully. He wished that he could spare her from the battle tomorrow but knew that short of dying, there was nothing that would stop her from being there. His heart swelled with love for this girl. He loved her above all else and would stop at nothing to protect her if things didn't go their way. He would die to save her and would do so willingly.

It felt weird sleeping at night, but they needed their strength to be at maximum peak for what was about to happen when the sun came up.

She opened her eyes and smiled when she saw him watching her. "Penny for your thoughts." She said. Matthew wanted to make love to her for what could be the last time. This time tomorrow, they could all be dead. He stood, lifted the covers, and got into the bed beside her. "I'd rather show you." He growled. His voice was full of lust. She reached up to his face and closed her eyes as their lips met in a passionate kiss. "I love you," she said.

Scene Fifty: Time

Marcus gently placed his finger under Tori's chin and lifted her face. "Maybe when this is over, we can get to know each other properly," he said. She reached up and tenderly placed her hand over his. "I'd like that," she whispered. "I do like an older man." He chuckled as he pulled her to him and kissed her lips. Both Ruth and Matthew smiled as they watched them.

Marcus looked around the room. "Come on then," he said, "let's get this over with."

Ruth's mobile phone rang. She picked it up, swiped the video icon upwards to accept Callie's call, and smiled when her cousin's face appeared on the screen.

"Hi Cal," she said as cheerily as she could muster, "is everything ok where you are?" "Yeah, we're all fine," she said, "Anna and the rest of the staff have been treating us like royalty. So what's happening where you are? Have there been any developments?"

"No, nothing," she lied, "we're still planning on what to do and how to go about it, but Cal, I don't want you to worry; Marcus has found a secret weapon that we can use to kill Isabella."

Ruth swallowed against the lump in her throat. At her request, Marcus had informed his staff that Beth, Jack, and Callie were not to be told of today's battle; She wanted to protect them as much as she possibly could, but if the worst happened and she died today, Anna Sommers had been asked to tell them of her death.

"Oh, that's wonderful news," Callie said, "Thank god he's on our side." Ruth watched

Marcus as he spoke excitedly to Mary Brunyee. He had done so much for her, and she would be eternally grateful to him. He had promised that, even if he didn't survive, his staff would take care of them financially for the rest of their lives.

"OK, I have to go now, Cal," she said, returning her attention back to the call with her cousin, "Matt and I have a training session in the gym. I'll speak to you later." Callie laughed, "try not to kick his ass too badly," she giggled, "and remember; We love you." Again, Ruth swallowed against the lump in her throat. "Love you too, cuz," she said, then ended the call.

Scene Fifty-One: Determination

Outside sat two large, blacked-out vans. One had been reversed up onto the pavement in front of Marcus' London home and was as close to the front door as was possible. His human helpers opened the back doors, and vampires left the house in a blur and landed unscathed in the back of the van. They closed the doors, and the van pulled and parked onto the road. Then, they did the same with the second vehicle for the remaining vampires.

Matthew squeezed Ruth's hand, and she smiled as she squeezed back. He remembered watching her fall from the tree when they had first ventured into the park for her first training session and smiled. He was so proud of her.

"Tomorrow," he said, "we can get Marcus' pilot to bring your family ba..." Cutting him off, she placed her finger over her lips. "Shh," she said. "I can't think that far ahead. What if we lose? They'll never be able to come home." Matthew tried to smile. "Well then," he said, "let's just make sure that we win then, shall we?"

Scene Fifty-Two: War

Vampires hid in the darkness of what was once a men's clothing store and spoke sentimental words to each other, just in case they didn't make it to nightfall. The whites of Marcus' knuckles showed through the skin as he curled his fist around the wooden stake in his pocket.

Severin Slovac appeared at his side. "Have you ever wondered what happens when we go?" He asked. Confused, Marcus looked at him for a few seconds. "What do you mean?" He asked, "go where." Severin smiled. He was by far the oldest vampire on the scene and had had a lot of time to time about his mortality. "You know." he continued, "when we go poof." He splayed his fingers in the air in front of him in a gesture of an exploding bomb. Despite the severity of what was about to take place, Marcus laughed. "No, not really," he chuckled, "and I'm not going to start now. We're going to win, Sev. I promise."

Severin laid one hand on Marcus' shoulder and held the other out toward him. "Just in case we don't get through this, I want to thank you for being a good friend to me." He said. Marcus took his hand and shook it. "Right back at you, buddy," he said, "If you hadn't helped me hide for all these years, Isabella would have killed me a long time ago, so, thank you for that, my friend."

Their attention was drawn to the road as two long, blacked-out stretch limousines approached and pulled into the disused parking area. A human driver got out, and opened the back passenger door, then held a huge umbrella over Isabella as she elegantly stepped from the car and hurried into the shade of an empty perfume shop across from where they stood. Other human drivers did the same for Freida Meyer, George Wadman, Isaac Callahan, and several other vampires who had accompanied her to the site.

Although she had been told that it was to be a meeting between herself and Marcus, he was surprised that she had chosen to bring only a few vampires with her for protection; Especially since Stephanie had told them that she suspected that someone had betrayed her. Surely she must have entertained the thought that this could possibly be an attempt on her life. However, he couldn't wait to see the look on her face when she realised that half of the vampires that stood behind her were really on his side.

Isabella turned, pulled down the hood of her cape, and teased her hair with her fingers. She smiled at the child she had parented two thousand years ago.

"Hello Marcus," she said, "It's been a while. I've missed you." Marcus looked over his shoulder, and Joseph Abrams and Mary

Brunyee appeared, holding tightly onto Ruth and Matthew as they mock struggled to break free.

"All I want is to come home and be by your side again like before," Marcus said, "I miss those days."

Isabella scoffed. "Oh, drop the act, would you. Do you take me for a complete fool Marcus?" She growled. "How dare you to presume that I would fall for this ruse. I am the mother of all but one, and you expect to fool me this easily?" She glared at Joseph and Mary. "You both will pay for this. You should have known better than to aid this fool in his vendetta." She said, pointing to Marcus.

Mary released Ruth's arm and stepped forward. "I'm not afraid of you," she said venomously, "almost everyone in the vampire community hates you with a passion. Even if you kill us all here today, you won't be able to rest. Never again will you ever be able to trust a single person who has the misfortune to be involved with you. From here on in, you will always be looking over your shoulder and waiting for the next uprising to unfold because I promise you, Isabella, it will."

Isabella smiled. She had always liked Mary's sass. "You would be wise to err on the side of caution," she said, "I've always known you had a massive pair of balls on you, Mary, so I will excuse your betrayal if you come to me, and stand by my side." Mary sneered. "Never," she said, "if you want me, then come the fuck over here and get me."

To their horror, Isabella smiled wickedly as she stepped out into the sun. Several vampires fell to their knees in sheer terror as she stood in the open sunlight. The smile never left her face as her arms theatrically reached out to her sides; She looked up at the sky, closed her eyes, and laughed maniacally. "As you all can see, I don't need anyone's help to defeat you," she said lowering her head, "unlike you, the sun is not my enemy."

She focused her gaze firmly on Matthew, then, in a blur, she moved, grabbed him by the arm, and dragged him out into the rays of the sun. Marcus, Tori, and several other vampires ran into the open and fought ferociously to help him break free, but she held onto him tightly. As they burned in the sunlight, they had no choice but to give up and run for cover, but they were quickly replaced by others who tried to help him.

George, Frieda, and Isaac completed their betrayal as they turned and destroyed the vampires loyal to Isabella. Now, the mother of all but one was truly on her own.

As the fight continued, Ruth appeared in a blur behind Isabella and jumped onto her back. Vampires looked on in disbelief as she was able to wrap her legs as tightly as she could around Isabella's waist, pull her head back, and bite into her throat. Isabella screamed in agony as well as fury; What Ruth had done was enough to make Isabella release her hold of Matthew, and she let go of him. He wanted to stay and help Ruth, but he had no choice but to scamper to the shadows for a few moments to heal.

Ruth screamed in agony as steam rose from her skin, but she refused to let it stop her and managed to drink some of Isabella's blood. She threw her head back and screamed as it coursed through her veins, but Matthew's Uno Parente quickly recovered and tossed her to the floor, then bent and picked her up by her hair. Ruth thrashed and fought as hard as she could to get away, but she was burning and had little chance of escaping. Finally, Isabella tossed her across the parking area, and her body slammed hard onto the side of a building. Chunks of bricks and debris came loose and fell to the floor as she landed.

In a blur, Peter Halsey ran out into the open and dragged Ruth back into the shadows so she could heal.

Matthew raced back out into the open and did exactly as Ruth had done a few moments before. He sank his fangs into Isabella's throat and, by some miracle, was able to draw a small amount of blood from her veins before she threw him to the ground.

Although Ruth and Matthew's bites had weakened her, Isabella was still strong. She lunged at him, grabbed hold of his head, and held it tightly to her chest.

"This will be the second time I've drunk from you, my love," she said, "and sadly, it will be the last." Isabella exposed her fangs and lowered her head to his throat when a voice she recognized screamed her name. Isabella dropped Matthew and stood to her full height when she saw Stephanie. A wry smile spread across her face when she saw the crossbow her lover held in her hands.

Mary and Tori fled from the shadows and dragged Matthew to safety.

Suddenly, George Wadman appeared behind Isabella. He held her arms behind her as Stephanie took aim. Her hands shook, but the crosshairs of her bow finally landed on Isabella's beautiful face as, with absolutely no concern, she allowed George to hold her there. Their eyes met, and for a moment, Stephanie paused. Isabella inclined her head to the side and smiled lovingly, and panic filled the air as Stephanie momentarily lowered the bow. "I forgive you for your betrayal." She said. "Come to me, my love." Then, in a blur, Stephanie wearing nothing but a hooded cloak for protection, ran into the sunlight.

A single tear fell onto her face as she lowered the bow and fired the arrow at point-blank range into the middle of Isabella's chest. At first, Isabella began to smile, but it was quickly replaced by fear as the splinters from Jesus' cross did their holy work and ended one of the most dangerous creatures on the planet.

George ran back to the shade as blisters covered her face. She clawed at her clothing and screamed in absolute agony. The air crackled with electricity as the skin peeled back from her face and exposed her skull; then, she disintegrated into dust particles.

Everyone watched in sheer and utter panic as they swirled and danced in the air for a few moments, then gathered together and formed into the shape of a terrible demon. It flapped its wings, flew high above them, and then exploded in a loud whoosh.

The ground shook as an otherworldly scream echoed from the surrounding buildings, then, in full-blown panic, Isabella's human helpers fled to her limousines, got in, and sped away as fast as they could.

Marcus sent his own human helpers in pursuit. If they were to continue living, they would have to be influenced to forget that their mistress ever existed, and he vowed to help them do just that.

He looked back at the battlefield and

watched as Stephanie threw back the hood from her robes. She held her arms out to either side of her and smiled as she looked up at the sky for the first time in over a hundred years. Matthew watched the spectacle, and all at once, a number of emotions coursed through his body, and he felt a massive wave of empathy for his one-time nemesis.

Their eyes met, and she nodded. He mouthed the words "thank you," and she inclined her head towards him in mutual respect before looking back up to the sky. Black, wispy smoke rose from her face and arms as her flesh burned. The skin curled as it peeled back from her skull and drifted away in the wind; then, she screamed and disintegrated into nothing.

The earth rumbled beneath their feet as they ran for the vehicles that had brought them here. Giant slabs of rock violently forced their way to the ground's surface and stood like huge monoliths. The walls of the surrounding buildings cracked, then split, and dust filled the air as they broke apart and fell to the ground as if an invisible wrecking ball had knocked them down.

No one made a sound as they watched the carnage from the safety of the vehicles. Marcus cried softly. "We did it, Ant," he whispered to himself, "I'm sorry that it took me over eight hundred years, brother, but you finally have the justice you deserve."

He dried his eyes with the back of his thumbs as the widest of grins spread across his handsome face. "We did it," he said. The van rocked as vampires hugged each other and wept. "Take us home," he shouted to the driver, "I think we all deserve a drink."

Goosebumps covered Ruth's entire body as the reality of what they had achieved nestled into her brain. "She's really gone," she said to Matthew, "we can finally live our lives without the threat of Isabella or anyone like her hanging over us." Matthew grinned as he pulled her to him. "I love you," he said. Tears brimmed in her eyes as she placed her hand on his face. "I love you too."

Epilogue

TWO AND A HALF THOUSAND MILES AWAY IN JERUSALEM

Ahmed Ishtar wiped the beads of sweat from his forehead with his sleeve and silently ran inside the entrance of the cave. He turned and looked back at the bodies he had left lying on the desert floor and was amazed that the blood pooling beneath them had already begun to dry in the blistering hot sun. The witch's guards had fought hard, but he was an expert swordsman and had dealt with them swiftly and efficiently.

Before she left to go back to England, his mistress, Isabella Marshond, had promised to grace him with the gift of vampirism. Moreover, she told him that if he succeeded in his task of finding her mother, he would earn a place by her side for the rest of eternity, so he had fought with passion and sheer determination.

The witch inside was powerful, and he knew that if she caught him, he would die a long and excruciating death, so taking care not to make a sound, he tiptoed into a narrow torch-lit tunnel that had been carved from the bedrock beneath the sand and hugged the wall with his back as he sidestepped his way further in.

After a few minutes, he paused. Echoes of the witch's vile chanting reached his ears, and he knew that he was close. Full of hatred, he continued further into the tunnel as it gently meandered deeper and deeper into the depths of the earth, the ceiling dipping so low in places that he had to get on his hands and knees, and crawl. He paused when he saw a large opening in the rock about thirty meters away. It was an entryway into the cavern that held the witch he was there to end.

He took a moment to regulate his breathing and readied himself to kill or to be killed, then stealthily made his way along the last stretch of corridor and to the cave mouth. He held his breath and peered around the corner.

Unaware of his presence, the witch stood at a crudely made, stone-tabled altar with her back to him. Her arms were raised above her head, and the coarse material of her robes gathered in a heap at her shoulders. His eyes widened when he saw a mass of black worms that had burrowed their way into her flesh. They writhed just beneath the skin; Undulating from one shape to another.

Magical symbols and words written in Adamic were carved deeply into the cavern's stone walls, and several small bones covered with engravings were scattered across the tabletop.

He sneered in hatred when her whispers

bounced from the walls of the cave as she chanted the powerful binding spell that continued to keep his goddess in captivity. He closed his eyes and mouthed a silent prayer to his beloved Lillith, the mother of all vampires, then carefully removed his blowpipe from its pouch and put the tube to his mouth. He blew as hard as he could, and the poison-loaded dart landed in her neck. Her knees buckled, and within seconds, dust particles dropped from the ceiling as the earth started to tremble. She turned and screamed his name as she reached out to grab him, but an invisible force picked her up and slammed her against the wall. Her piercing red eyes dulled as the poison raged through her body, then glazed over in death.

He scrambled back through the tunnels until he came to the mouth of the cave and fell to his knees on the desert floor. Grains of sand bounced around his face as the earth continued to tremble. Then, a loud crack filled the air as the ground opened up, and a large chasm appeared. Movement came from below.

The air pulsated as Lillith, In the form of a terrifying demon, burst out from the opening. The wind shifted around her as her wings beat the air. She peered down, and when her gaze landed on Ishtar, she picked him up in her claw, curled her talons around him, and removed his head from his body with just one bite. She threw back her head and screamed one word. "Ismaliiiaaaa."

END OF BOOK THREE

I hope from the bottom of my heart that you enjoyed reading "War", If so, can I ask you if you would be kind enough to write a (hopefully favorable) review for me?

Search on Amazon for
'War Book Three in The Vampire Ruth Series'

Thank you so very much

Lea X

Book Four in The Vampire Ruth Series

Available Soon

About the Author

Lea Davies is originally from southeast London but now lives in Kent, the garden of England with her husband. She has two strapping sons, and two wonderful grandchildren who she loves and adores.

Other Books by Lea Davies

Book One in The Vampire Ruth Series: The Gift

Book Two in The Vampire Ruth Series: Choices

For more information on the books and

characters, visit leadavies.com

Printed in Great Britain
by Amazon